P9-AQQ-695

# HEAT

## ALSO BY WILLIAM GOLDMAN

### FICTION

*The Temple of Gold* (1957)
*Your Turn to Curtsy, My Turn to Bow* (1958)
*Soldier in the Rain* (1960)
*Boys and Girls Together* (1964)
*No Way to Treat a Lady* (1964)
*The Thing of It Is . . .* (1967)
*Father's Day* (1971)
*The Princess Bride* (1973)
*Marathon Man* (1974)
*Magic* (1976)
*Tinsel* (1979)
*Control* (1982)
*The Color of Light* (1984)

### NONFICTION

*The Season: A Candid Look at Broadway* (1969)
*The Making of "A Bridge Too Far"* (1977)
*Adventures in the Screen Trade: A Personal View of Hollywood and Screenwriting* (1983)

### SCREENPLAYS

*Masquerade* (1965)
(with Michael Relph)
*Harper* (1966)
*Butch Cassidy and the Sundance Kid* (1969)
*The Hot Rock* (1972)
*The Great Waldo Pepper* (1975)
*The Stepford Wives* (1975)
*All the President's Men* (1976)
*Marathon Man* (1976)
*A Bridge Too Far* (1977)
*Magic* (1978)
*Mr. Horn* (1979)

### PLAYS

*Blood, Sweat, and Stanley Poole* (1961)
(with James Goldman)
*A Family Affair* (1962)
(with James Goldman and John Kander)

### FOR CHILDREN

*Wigger* (1974)

# William Goldman

# HEAT

A Warner Communications Company

Warner Books, Inc., 666 Fifth Avenue, New York, NY 10103

A Warner Communications Company

Printed in the United States of America
First Printing: May 1985
10 9 8 7 6 5 4 3 2 1

**Library of Congress Cataloging in Publication Data**

Goldman, William, 1931–
Heat.

I. Title.
PS3557.0384H4 1985 813'.54 84-40656
ISBN 0-446-51275-3

*Designed by Giorgetta Bell McRee*

*For Carlin and*
*Carlos and*
*Gerri and*
*Dave*

*Knick fans all*

# HEAT

# PART I

# The Mex

# CHAPTER 1

# Holly and the All-Black Night

At least nothing was broken.

She knew that. No. The savaging had been so sudden, the imparting of pain so skilled, that she knew precious little.

But nothing was broken; she sensed that.

And she so wanted it to be true. Because that would mean she was looking on the bright side, the last words her father had spoken to her, the last words and the first advice. "Holly," he'd said, "I can't leave you money but I can give you gold: You be sure you always look on the bright side. No matter how bad a thing is, there's gotta be one part that's brighter than the other. There's never yet been an all-black night. So you keep an eye out for that bright side and you'll always be okay."

I'll always be okay, Holly told herself.

Not in so many words, of course. Not in words at all. Probably it was some feeling triggered by the part of you that remembered things.

What part was that?

She lay there and searched for the answer. Lay where? Someplace hard. Hard and jagged. Steps? Yes. More than likely.

The brain! That was the part of you that did the remembering. Gold star, Holly.

Gold stars belonged to her mother. She owned the only ones that counted anywhere in all the world and she was *very* careful when it came to doling them out. If your room was perfect, *perfect,* then you got a whole complete gold star. Holly tried, so hard, and once she got a half but that was the best. She would slave over her room or the dishes or her schoolwork or her baby-sitting jobs, always sweet no matter how monstrous the brat, but she never got more than a half star. "Someday you'll be my gold-star girl," her mother would say when Holly's heart was near to breaking, when she'd slaved at some chore or other and come up short. "If it was easy, anybody could be a gold-star girl and then who'd want to be one?"

I would, I would, Holly used to think, but she never said it.

"There are precious few gold-star girls," her mother would say, "but I do believe you have the makings. And then, *then*, my baby, you'll always be special."

I'll always be special, Holly told herself.

Not in so many words, of course. Not in words at all. Probably it was some feeling triggered by . . . by . . . *your brain.*

You got it that time, Holly, gold star, Holly, you've come up with the answer without even much of a pause, which has to mean you're looking on the bright side and getting better and better.

Holly lay very still on the hard steps and closed her eyes, with one question causing her such confusion: If she was getting better and better, then why was she leaking worse and worse?

And she was. She was definitely leaking. Blood.

She opened her eyes. She was watching the ceiling. Below her vision, something was moving. She forced her eyes down from the ceiling. She could see the moving things now and they were piggies. No. Piggies were what went to market and they belonged way below at the bottom of you. These were like piggies except they went on your . . . *hands.*

"Fingers" was the word she was looking for. Fingers were what she was looking at. Hers? Yes. More than likely. She bent the arm that connected the fingers to the rest of her and began to search for leaks.

First the fingers touched the eyes. Then the fingers moved away so the eyes could look at them. The fingers looked like fingers. That meant the eyes weren't leaking. But the nose was. She touched the nostrils, moved the fingers away so the eyes could look at them. The fingers were red and wet now. The mouth was leaking, too, when she touched it. Not the whole mouth. Just the lips. They were leaking badly, she could feel the blood wet through the skin, she didn't need to move the fingers away and give the eyes a chance.

I'll always be okay, Holly told herself. A few slits had been opened but they would close, because that's all slits ever did, if you looked on the bright side.

Only she could sense other leaks. Worse ones. She closed her eyes again and thought about the bright side and moved her fingers down her dress (her "party dress" her mother would have called it, her very best one) and the collar of the dress was fine, it felt just like it should—

—but the bodice didn't. It was all ripped and torn and Holly reached for her breasts. She never wore a bra; even now at thirty there had never been the need—she had always been small, but she had always been firm. Her breasts were tender but that didn't bother her one bit. What did was that her nipples were leaking. She raised her hand, let her reopened eyes examine the fingers. Red and moist.

For just a moment Holly thought it might be hard to find the bright side. Tears were never even a remote possibility. Holly did not cry. Did not ever do that. Crying meant there wasn't a bright side and that simply couldn't be true.

Now she had it—who cared if her nipples were torn—they would heal, that's what tears did. And how many women her age could say, "No, I've never worn a bra and it's not 'cause I'm built like a boy, either."

One last leak to go.

Holly used her left hand for the first time, fresh fingers, hesitated, hesitated, then moved them down, down to her "special place" (her mother had called it that), touched herself, outside and briefly, because the pain was so bad, in.

The worst leak of all. I need a bright side, Holly thought. I do, I need one, I need one *now,* please, please. . . .

This was a toughie. Finding a star in what seemed more and more like an all-black night. Wait—wait—it was right there all the time. How many women her age could say, "No, I've never worn a bra and it's not 'cause . . ."

Holly almost shook her head. She would have if she could have. She'd made a mistake, come up with a *wrong* bright side. It didn't have anything to do with her "special place," and besides, she'd already used it.

And then, just when she thought she might be a damsel who would never be able to get out of her distress because she was trapped in a dungeon with no bright side, Holly's Galahad appeared, speaking in a strange tongue:

b r
y t e e e e
u n b h l e
u a e n a d
c e y

Not your garden variety Galahad, no question about that. Holly made her eyes focus on him as he knelt beside her. His skin was black and his clothes were gold. Not clothes really, more a costume; no, a uniform, and across the chest was stitched the word CROESUS. Now again, the foreign tongue:

b r
y t e e e e
u n b h l e
u a e n a d
c e y

Holly closed her eyes tightly because part of being crazy was just thinking that you were that, *and she wasn't*. Now *think*! CROESUS meant The Croesus Hotel. So that was where she was. On some steps in The Croesus Hotel. And he was speaking English, plain, ordinary English—no—black English, but that wasn't what was throwing her, it was that she couldn't stop the sound from washing over her in waves.

Holly did her best to still the waters. "Yuu" was "you." "Cant" was just "can't" without the apostrophe. Good work so far: "You can't." Keep going.

"Be" was obvious. "Be."

"Been" was a toughie but she got it. He meant "being." Then she had it all: "You can't be being here, lady." Some tasks seemed so hard, but they weren't, not if you kept plugging. And she had. Gold star, Holly.

Now he shook her. She made a groan. He stopped shaking her. Next he tried lifting her. Her dead weight was too much. He stopped trying to lift her.

"Lady, you got to get up, get out, moooove, y'unnerstan? These here service stairs are for us service people."

Holly understood, she just didn't know how to do much about it.

The black man—busboy? room service?—stood up. "I'll get Security, you stay right here," and he was gone.

When her "f-a-c-u-l-t-i-e-s were intact"—(Salinger, *For Esme, With Love and Squalor*—a quote, so she must be getting better)—when her faculties were intact, she was not without humor and the black man saying "You stay right here" when all in the world she was capable of doing *was* staying right there, well, there must be a joke in that vicinity—and suddenly she knew the bright side that had worried her so just before—if she could think of the existence of a joke, that meant she wasn't going to die, maybe the brightest side of all. . . .

The security man was grey-haired and also had the same

word, CROESUS, stitched across his uniform. He carried an old sheet, knelt beside her.

"She can't move too good on her own." That was the voice of Galahad, from above, the waves gone now. Holly couldn't speak, not out loud, not yet, but she could understand. Some. Holly looked more closely at the grey-haired security man. He had a caring face. Like Joel McCrea. And long gentle hands and he held the old sheet gently. "I don't want none of this cunt's blood fucking up my uniform," he said as he rolled Holly into the sheet.

So much for Joel McCrea.

As her body spun into the cloth Holly began to lose it again. She was on her feet. His arm held her roughly to his body. "All clear?"

"Floor's empty." This had to still be Galahad.

"Can't have the customers seeing shit like this."

Now Holly was rising. Up the service steps. Pause. Across the hotel corridor to the service elevator, the door propped open. In. The prop removed. The doors whooshed shut. Down. To the . . . to the . . . Holly tried to make out the elevator button that was lit. S.B.

She would have known that once. Right off.

The door to the elevator opened and there were concrete pillars and cars and a man standing close by. "Take her to Memorial, drop her at the emergency entrance. This car got a hotel marking?"

"No."

"Okay. Drop her and get your ass back here. Drag her out when you get there, she can't move so good on her own."

Then the back door was pulled open. And Holly was thrown on the floor. And the car moved, the sound of the motor roaring in the cement subbasement. That must have been what "S.B." meant. Now the roaring was less. They were out of the cement surroundings and into the night. Turn. Turn. (For every something . . . turn turn . . . there is a season, turn . . . turn . . . turn . . .)

She was covered by the sheet now, her face, body; nothing protruded. The bumping of the car on the road as the driver gunned along, that hurt. She was facedown and her swollen lips got worse every time they bumped, her swollen nose too.

Very dazed now.

Time sense gone.

Stop. Front door opens. Then hers opens. Then hands pull at her. Then the sheet is off and she is on the ground. Ground cold. Car drives away. Lights. Long word. "Emergency"? Please, God. Crawl. Toward long word. Knees hurt now but long word important, must reach long word.

She almost did. Her strength gave out just before she got there. But then there was a man. An orderly. And he began to shout. And then there was a chair. A chair with wheels. And she was whizzing along until there was a bed, and the orderly put her on the bed and then two men appeared, in white robes, doctors, and a white curtain was pulled around the bed so there could be privacy and Holly, safe, looked to find the strength for speech.

"...mmm..." she said. "...meh..."

"What's she trying to say?" the first doctor asked. He put his ear close to her leaking mouth.

Holly tried again, again, kept on.

"Well?" from the second doctor, standing straight.

"No sense," the first doctor answered. "Sounds like she's saying 'the Mex' over and over."

"My guess," the second doctor said—and he spoke with the authority of someone who had earned a Ph.D. in bloodshed—"my very good guess is that 'the Mex' is the Mexican gentleman who done this to her."

# CHAPTER 2

# D.D. Before Dawn

As soon as she walked into the empty place and saw the big Mexican sitting alone on a barstool, D.D. was something she usually wasn't: afraid.

She couldn't figure why. She didn't know for sure if he was a Mex or not—except he had the same kind of killer looks Pancho Gonzales had when he was pushing forty. Her old man was a Gonzales nut—"greatest human to ever hit a ball"—and he took her once to some crummy exhibition. It didn't mean spit, it was all show business, but halfway through the match Gonzales got a bad bounce, lost a point—

—and D.D.'s heart stopped.

Because he stared down, Gonzales did, stared at the offending ground and then he raised his racket high over his head, hatchet-style, and he froze a moment—

—and in that moment D.D., bewitched by the dark power in that arm, by the blazing eyes and the face that seemed to say to women, "I can have any goddam one of you and *we both* know it"—in that frozen moment of wild frustration D.D. knew beyond doubt that had Gonzales chosen to attack the earth with his racket edge, that the earth would have had no choice but to split cringing beneath the superior force that had been unleashed against it.

On the court that day, Gonzales regained control, went back to his position for the next point. For D.D. in the stands, no matter where Gonzales went that day, in her mind he was still in that frozen moment, racket raised, a king beyond fury.

Now, in the bar, the guy who looked like Pancho Gonzales

was watching her in the mirror, and maybe he was smiling, it was dark, they weren't that close, you couldn't be sure.

Then he spun in his barstool and there wasn't much mistake possible so D.D. quickly checked her watch. Five 'til four.

The Mex was still watching her.

D.D. stared out at the night, wondering if she should go wait in the car rather than inside this goddam rat trap, but that was dumb: If there was one thing about Osgood Percy, you could count on him. If he said he'd meet her at four, she had only five minutes to get through on her own, and she was a big girl.

A very big girl.

Especially there, where the Mex was staring now. She couldn't help being zaftig, goddammit. They started sprouting when she was eleven, so go blame God.

No; not entirely true. She dressed to make men look. In the beginning it was a kick, watching the way they watched her while they pretended otherwise. She liked the way their wives stared at their husbands staring at her.

But now. Why was she dressed the way she was dressed, close-fitting skirt, white sweater tucked in tight, a wide black belt setting off the whole frame? Jesus, that was dumb, she didn't have to *get* the interest of Osgood Percy, she had too much of his interest as it was. That was why, for this, what he called "the most important talk either of them would ever have," he picked this dump outside town, because in town there was no privacy in the public places and in the private places, his apartment or hers, the look of her drove him crazy, he couldn't talk about anything but how he loved her, couldn't do anything but make passes that she either fought off or surrendered to, depending on how whipped she was from the running she'd had to do carrying drinks at the Golden Nugget.

3:56 A.M. now. D.D. walked to the farthest end of the bar, got the attention of the old bartender, who was dozing, ordered a Diet Pepsi, paid, took it to the farthest booth in the deepest corner of the place, sat heavily down.

3:59.

Osgood Percy, dear God. What in the world was her answer going to be?

You could go crazy listing his virtues. So honest, upright and true, you could pitch. Brave, clean, reverent.

And he worshiped her.

Not so terrible, not so far.

He wasn't bad looking. Not homely anyway. He stood five eight, an inch more than her. His weight was a trim 155. Never varied more than a pound: He wouldn't let it.

Smart. Kind of funny too. No Rickles, but he could come up with a good line more often than you gave him credit for. And he *appreciated* a laugh, which was a plus in anybody's book.

His career was solid and heading noplace else but up—it was his goddam career that brought on this "most important talk of their lives" moment, which was coming up fast on the outside.

One past four. D.D. sipped her Diet Pepsi. With an ordinary human, one minute late you didn't think about. But with Osgood Percy, it was odd.

D.D. had an insight then and this is what it was: Even when she was alone and noodling on about him, she thought of him as "Osgood Percy." Not "Oz." Or "Ozzie." Or "Goody" or "Perce." Nope—it was the whole name.

The whole horrible name.

The whole horrible formal name.

That was the nutshell—the best man she'd ever met, the most decent human being who had ever had the hots for her at least, and he wasn't a nerd but you didn't think you were humping Errol Flynn when he was inside you. Not that he was bad at it. You couldn't concentrate on recipes while he was slip-sliding away.

He was just, kind of, well, too formal. He never lost

control, went wild, thrilled her, thrilled himself, too self-conscious—

—probably his fucking wig.

If there was one thing worse than Osgood Percy's name, it was that. He was all the time touching it, seeing that it hadn't gone scooting off anywhere since the last touch, ten seconds maybe sooner.

It was a nice wig. Black and short. It was an expensive wig. Perfect fit. If only he'd had left the goddam thing alone more, you maybe might not have had proof positive he was wearing one.

But he couldn't leave it alone. *Could not.*

D.D. remembered the ghastly half hour near the end of their first month of dating when he, blushing with such sad eyes, told her, in case she hadn't guessed, that he wasn't as young as he might seem, he was thirty-eight but that was because of . . . the . . . that was because of the . . . "There mustn't be secrets between us. . . ."

*RUG,* D.D. wanted to scream. *Your fucking scalp doily.* Only, of course, she didn't, didn't come close, he was hurting so bad, cared so much for her. He had spotted her her first night in Vegas, before she was sure she was even going to stay, when she was wandering through Caesars, where he was a pit boss. He asked if he could see her later. He was important. She said yes. Later he asked if she had a job. She said no. He got her one. Downtown at the Golden Nugget, taking orders from the bar to the gamblers.

She owed him so much that when he finally got it out—"My hair . . . D.D. . . . it's real but only some of it, you better know that now"—she didn't fake it. "I don't give a damn, *you*'re real, all of you, that's what *I* care about."

White lies could get you into deep shit and that was God's truth.

Four-oh-*five.*

D.D. looked around, concerned, confused and then afraid, as behind her now, moving toward her, drunk but doing a decent job of hiding it, was the Mex. She turned back to her table. He was as big as she'd guessed—six three, solid, close to two hundred, powerful arms, muscular shoulders. He was probably hung, too, D.D. thought, wishing her mind didn't work that way, but what the hell could you do when you were thirty-five, stacked, three times divorced, always to hunks, studs, stallions.

"Coulda fooled me," he said when he stood by her booth.

D.D. stared down at her Diet Pepsi, said nothing. He didn't talk like any South-of-the-Border sleaze. No accent she could trace anyway. 'Course he was boozed pretty good, but he was hiding it okay. As she sat there silently, D.D. wished she hadn't taken such an out-of-the-way place to sit. Nearer the bartender would have been a smarter move. The bartender was old, but at least he'd be closer to the phone to call for help in case trouble broke out.

She glanced up at the man who looked like a young Pancho Gonzales, then away, her fear deeper now.

Because trouble *was* going to break out. He wanted it, she was good at telling that. Hell, she shoulda been, after three husbands whose idea of a good time was to beat up on somebody. That was why she felt afraid when she walked in: Violence had a musk all its own.

"Coulda fooled me all ri'," he said again, standing there, holding a full glass of dark liquid in his hand. "You looked like the kind enjoys a good time."

*Eight* minutes after—step on it, Osgood Percy, please.

"Second you come in here I said to myself, 'That's a girl who enjoys a good time.' "

"I enjoy a good time," D.D. said.

"On Diet Pepsi?" he said, and put the glass he was holding on the table in front of her. "See, I asked the bartender to gimme one of whatever you were havin' so I could bring it over. I figured you for a Seven and Seven. When he gimme a *soft* drink . . ." He shrugged his big shoulders. "I was surprised, y'know what I mean?" He looked at the empty ashtray. "Don't smoke either?"

D.D. shook her head.

"No vices, huh?"

"I got plenty vices, I just don't drink or smoke," D.D. said while inside she was going, 'Are you whacko?—are you out of your goddamn gourd?—*stop talking to this guy before he gets the wrong idea.*' No. He already *had* the wrong idea. What she had to do was stop encouraging him.

He stepped closer to the table, began to move his pelvis very slightly, back and forth, back and forth. "Let's hear about them vices." He smiled down at her.

"Look, Mister—my boyfriend's overdue and thanks for the drink and all, but please, it's very important that I have some time—I got a lot of heavy thinking to do."

"Oh, I would never want to intrude," he said, almost laughing but holding it back. "Just tell me your name and I'm gone forever. 'I need your name so I can put it to your frame'—little pome, y'see? When I think of you walkin' in wearing that white sweater, I need a name to go along. You're a succulent lady and I'll bet I know your vices."

"D.D."

"Your *name,* I said, no initials shit." He put a big hand over his mouth in mock embarrassment. "'Scuse—prob'ly you don't swear, neither."

"It is my name. My official name, I mean it."

"Don't make sense."

"It would if you knew my mother—she was a Doris Day nut and she was pregnant with me . . ." D.D. stopped, he had her scared almost into telling the truth, which was that it was Doris Day's first movie in the late forties that made her mother decide. If she admitted that and you could add, you'd know she was thirty-five, not the twenty-eight she admitted to. "She saw Doris Day in some middle-fifties flick—almost thirty years ago—and decided what to call me then. Okay, now you know about my name, g'bye."

"Bye, D.D.," he said, and just before he turned he added, "Y'know what I think?"

D.D. shook her head.

"I think you and me, we had a shot at something."

He went back to the bar then, and when she was sure it would go undetected, D.D. threw a look at his retreating body. A swagger—she knew it—he walked like John Wayne, big and slow with a lot of wiggle in the ass.

She looked down then at her two Diet Pepsis. At least she was alone (at least for *now* she was alone, but who knew how long before the spick got the itch again?). D.D. figured her choices. She could call Caesars and ask for Osgood Percy, only that was bad because the phone was up near where the Pepsi Bringer sat, drinking alone, and if she went near him there was no way he wouldn't figure she was *interested.* Or she could go sit alone in her car in the dark lot, but that was bad, too, because he'd follow her out there, she *knew* that.

The best thing to do, of course, was just to get the hell out and into her car and drive home, and that's what she wanted to do, would have done—

—except Osgood Percy would be crushed, when he got there, that she had taken off and left before "the most important talk either of them would ever have."

Was it really all that important?

Yeah, D.D. had to admit, probably it was. Shit, but it was. The future was what the talk was going to hinge on, *their* future, hers and Osgood Percy's. Or, more precisely, would there be one?

It had all blown up fast, just a couple weeks before. He was this pit boss at Caesars, he ran a roulette pit, he was in charge of roulette tables and the Caesars people asked would he change assignments and become a pit boss in their Atlantic City place?

But underneath their query was an unstated fact: that soon, if he did the job well—and he would, he loved casino work—they would advance him up to being *shift* boss—which meant he would be responsible for the entire gambling operation for one of the three eight-hour shifts of one of the giant gambling hotels in the world while still under forty. He was going, clearly, all the way.

D.D.'s problem was, forget about going all the way, Osgood Percy wouldn't even go to Atlantic City unless she came along.

Tomorrow was his deadline to tell them yes or no. Tonight was her deadline to tell him yes or no.

He was decent about it, like he was always decent, Osgood Percy. It wouldn't destroy him if he stayed in Vegas. Eventually, he'd get up to the top. Sure, it would take more time, years maybe, but what the hell good was his time if he had to spend it without her?

In all her life, D.D. had never sunk the hook as deep into a man as this one. She sensed it while it was happening, was kind of interested in watching the results. She personally wasn't much into S & M, but there was kind of a fascination with having a slave, just this once.

And she liked Osgood Percy. Truly, truly. But Atlantic City was in *New Jersey,* for Chrissakes, which meant ice, winter, and she was a hothouse child, born and bred in San Diego, who took vacations in Hawaii. Two of her husbands had been from Hawaii. She had planned her life as much as possible to avoid the cold.

But there was more than the weather involved, because underneath Osgood Percy's insistence that she move with him was the unspoken fact that she move *in* with him. And after that she knew what he wanted—

—don't toss your cookies: love.

And after love?—

—head for the railing and lean way out: marriage.

And the terrible truth?

D.D. wasn't sure what her answer would be. Vegas was action and Vegas was warm, but Vegas was also working her buns off at the Golden Nugget. And the insults and the propositions and all the rest of the downtown Fremont Street crud.

Atlantic City was probably action and definitely freezing. But she wouldn't have to work. Osgood Percy said that was out. It was a new start and her decorating whatever place they rented in whatever style she liked, and once he made shift boss, it meant your man had Power. Your man was headed for very big things and wouldn't that be a helluva ride after three husbands whose total earnings, all three together in their best years, didn't come to thirty thousand? A failed football player, a snorkling teacher, a body-builder who pushed vitamins door to door when he wasn't looking in the mirror. (The first was the boy next door—down the block, really—in San Diego who she'd lost it to, the others her Hawaiian wonders.)

Jesus, D.D. wondered, do I flip a coin for my life, heads it's here, tails it's Jersey? What was the answer, what in the world was going to come out of her mouth when Osgood Percy was sitting across from her, looking at her with all that love on his face underneath the black rug he was all the time fingering?

"He must sure have . . . have all the ass he . . . wants."

D.D., so lost in herself, blinked.

The Mex was back, drunker than before, standing close to the table, looking down. "Man stands up a . . . a piece—no insult 'tended, y'unnerstan'?—but a man—this 'boyfriend' that's making you . . . do this 'heavy thinkin' '—he must have 'em waiting in line. 'Sumin', 'course, that there's a 'he' and you weren't bullshitting, I mean, it is going on four-thirty."

Four-thirty! D.D. couldn't believe her watch. But she believed every bit of anger in the swarthy drunk's eyes. She did what she always did when she was really frightened; tried to tough it through. "He exists and he'll be here, I don't have to do any bullshitting, all right?"

The Mex wasn't retreating in panic—"Let's dance."

*"What?"*

He opened a big hand, held it out for her. "C'mon—jes' you and me."

D.D. shook her head. "This isn't a place for dancing—it's illegal."

"I slipped the old fart a couple bucks, he don't care what we do. Whatever you like, I'll put it on the juke."

D.D. said nothing.

"The Stones. You like the Stones?"

Silence.

"YOU MUST LIKE SOMEBODY, FOR CHRISSAKES."

Whispered: ". . . Manilow . . ."

"Okay, I'll put on a Manilow."

"I don't want to dance, I really truly don't, I'm not in the mood, please."

"Maybe you'll be in the mood later."

Silence.

"ANSWER ME."

"Maybe later, sure."

"'Later.' That's our own private password, y'unnerstan'?"

"Right, right, you got it," D.D. said, not giving a damn what her words were because as the Mex left her alone again she saw a car roar into the lot and park next to hers and then Osgood Percy was dashing inside. Right then, wig and all, he looked, D.D. thought, very much like a keeper.

He stopped in the doorway, spotted her, half ran to her booth, going "I'm sorry, I'm sorry, I'm sorry, it's been a nightmare," and sat down across, took her hands.

"Let's get out of here," D.D. said.

"Doris, I just arrived," Osgood Percy said, and his blue eyes looked at her in surprise.

Why did she keep forgetting his blue eyes? D.D. wondered. She'd always been a sucker for blue. Only one of her first three had had blue eyes, the only one Osgood Percy knew about; she told him she was divorced, what was the point of too much detail anyway?

And the way he called her "Doris" sometimes. No one else ever had and she liked it. Why did she keep forgetting that too?

"There's a drunk who's been hitting on me, let's take off and go to my place before something happens."

"I'm here, and nothing's going to happen. And please remember why *we*'re here—I don't want to make a pass at you and I don't want to get to thinking about how I feel about you—I want to talk rationally, human to human, without distractions, yes?"

She hesitated, made a nod. "I feel better with you around."

"I'm flattered to hear that, and if that were always the case, we wouldn't have a problem—but I suspect what you mean is 'I feel better with you around *right now*' because you're a beautiful woman and you were alone and some drunk scared you."

"You're too smart for me. Don't deny it."

"(A) I don't want to get sidetracked, I'm not too smart for you and let's drop that line of conversation, because it's not what we're here for, and (B) you wouldn't think I was smart at all if you knew why I was late."

"Tell me."

"You're trying to sidetrack me again, Doris, now please, can it."

"Just shorthand it for me and then we'll get right to business. I promise. It's not like you to be a second late, forget half an hour. So you do kind of owe me an explanation."

Osgood Percy sat back in the booth and folded his slender hands with the perfectly manicured fingernails. "Two Saudis—princes, I imagine—young and dumb and drunk and they lost over three quarters of a million waiting for double zero to come up. I mean, you can't believe how they were pissing their money away, not that it matters to them, they've got so much. And they were enjoying it until it came time to switch shifts and I was thinking, believe me, of you, when suddenly they got nasty, they claimed they were being cheated, all of us were in on it, they demanded to see the casino manager, so in we trooped to his office and since it was my immediate responsibility he asked me to explain and I was so hysterical worrying about you waiting alone out here I couldn't do it—I was like some incoherent schmuck trying to give a speech in high school class when you haven't done your homework. Eventually, everything got smoothed out, but it took a while, which is where I've been and—"

"It's 'later,'" the big Mexican said, making his drunken way to the booth.

From the jukebox now, Barry Manilow was singing "I Write the Songs."

Osgood Percy looked up at the much bigger man, took a deep breath, said, "We're talking."

"It's our *password,* asshole," the Mex said, and he held out his hand toward D.D. "Manilow, just like you wanted."

Osgood Percy stared at D.D., waited.

"I only said it to get rid of him, I said maybe later we'd dance, anything to make him go away."

"All right?" Osgood Percy said, looking up.

The drunk looked stupefied for a moment. "All right? A girl says yes, she wants to dance with me and you come along and get her to change her mind and you wonder if it's all right? You fucking nuts? *It's all wrong!*" He grabbed D.D. by one wrist, started to pull. "Now, c'mon!"

D.D. used everything she had and yanked free.

The Mex took several steps back before he had his balance again. He smiled at D.D. "Strong," he said. "That's a plus in my book. I like it when women start out strong 'cause when I'm done with 'em, they're kinda weak, think you'll like that, D.D.?"

"You told him your *name*?" Osgood Percy said.

"I hadda get rid of him, I explained that to you."

"What else did you tell him while I was getting pissed on by some Saudi punk?"

Now the Mex was moving back. "She tole me a lot—like how you're all the time whining, and how you can't get it up. She tole me plenty, right, D.D.?"

"Aw shit," D.D. said, shaking her head.

Osgood Percy reached over, patted her hand. Then he stared up at the dark drunk. "Your time is up, we have to talk, good-bye."

The Mex almost giggled, took a step closer to the booth.

Osgood Percy stared up at the bigger man. "I don't think you want to make me mad," he said.

D.D. watched, and if you didn't know Osgood Percy, you would have gone along with the hard look on his face. But she knew him and in his voice, no matter how much he tried to bury it, she could hear it: the very slight hesitation, the dry throat, the fear.

"I don't care what games you two wanna play," D.D. said. "I'm getting the hell out," and she started to rise.

"Don't think so," the Mex said, and he shoved her back down into the booth. "We got our 'later' coming up soon—you an' me an' Manilow."

"That's twice you've touched her," Osgood Percy said. "This is a warning: Don't do it again. All right?"

The Mex raised his hands to shoulder level, palms forward. "I won't touch her again," he said. He paused. "'Til she asks me." He winked at D.D. "But I got one question."

Osgood Percy waited.

"The one thing I wanna know is . . ." the Mex began. And then he was shouting: *"Is it okay if I touch you?"* And with that he reached out one giant hand, placed it suddenly on Osgood Percy's head, and ripped the wig off.

The move came so quickly, was so unexpected, that D.D. didn't have time to take her eyes away and as she watched, Osgood Percy turned instantly red, his eyes flicked toward hers, and then he was looking down while D.D. said sadly, she couldn't help it, the words were there too fast: "Aw, Osgood," nothing all that damning, except in her tone was that what she saw now sitting across from her was a too-neat, small-boned man who couldn't stop blushing—not a keeper at all, not just now.

The Mex was waving the wig in front of him now as he backed away from the booth toward the area that was filled with rectangular wooden tables. He seemed very happy as he went "Nyah-nyah-ee—nyah-nyah," like kids used to do on the playground.

Osgood Percy got to his feet, still red, started toward the other man. "You give me that," he said.

"Come 'n' get it," the Mex said, backing away.

"That's mine and I want it!"

"It's right here," the Mex said, waving it above his head, then holding it out, shaking it. "Does it bite?" He began to laugh then, a great drunken roar.

"You be careful with that," Osgood Percy said, and then he moved quickly toward the Mex, who backed around a table, and when Osgood Percy lunged the Mex was six feet away, still laughing.

D.D., stunned, stared at the two men, and seeing them both standing it was like watching a grown man about to enter combat with a well-dressed boy.

The Mex backed through the mass of tables, waving the wig, taunting and laughing as he easily evaded Osgood Percy, who seemed stiff when compared to the drunken moves of the darker man.

Now they both stopped, frozen, a table between them. The Mex held out the wig as far as he could so that it was close enough for Osgood Percy to grab, and he tried, but he was too slow again, and his hand clenched on air as the big man backed off and tried very hard to stop laughing.

D.D. could see her date taking a quick look toward her

and he was blushing still, but now he seemed to be gathering himself for a greater effort, perhaps a final one, and D.D. was out of the booth then, running toward him, because the only thing that had kept him in a single piece was the fact that the Mex dodged too well and they had never quite been able to close in combat, and when she was in the table area D.D. called his name sharply and he looked at her, which gave her time to reach him and take his hands and say, "Please, please, get me outta here."

Osgood Percy looked at her for a moment before he said, "That cost a lot of money, it was made special."

"Fuck the money, Osgood."

"Osgood?" the giant said. "*Ozzz*-good? Nobody got a name called Ozzzzzzz-good."

D.D. moved up close and whispered, "He doesn't want the wig, he's just a bully, leave him alone and he'll get bored with it, that's how bullies think, they're only into trouble."

Osgood Percy hesitated.

D.D. didn't want to embarrass him any further so she went very close to his ear and said, so soft, "I'm scared—please—think of me a little, willya?—I want outta here, Osgood, help me."

Osgood Percy nodded. "In that case," he said, and he took a deep breath, reached for her arm, took it, began to steer her toward the distant door of the empty bar.

"Faster, huh?" D.D. told him. "I'm scared real bad." They picked up their pace, moving quickly away from the tables, past the old bartender, who sat watching their retreat.

"Don't be afraid," Osgood Percy said, and he gave her arm a squeeze.

"I can't help it, it's him," D.D. said, and she glanced back toward where the big Mex stood, watching them go.

"I could have taken care of him," Osgood Percy said.

"I know," D.D. answered, quickly.

"I don't like to make a big deal out of it, but I'm very good with my fists."

"Of course," D.D. said. "In your line of work, you have to be."

"That's right. When you start as a dealer on Fremont, you better be able to handle your dukes or you'll never last."

D.D. pushed hard at the glass door, and it opened and then they were outside, heading toward their cars. Hers was small and cheap, a secondhand tan Chevette, while he drove an English car, a Rover, not because it was flashy but rather, naturally, because it had an excellent record for traffic safety.

Now they were silent in the cold night. Their cars were ten yards off, the entrance to the bar was ten yards back. We're in the middle, D.D. thought, but she didn't want to think of what. She glanced at Osgood Percy, who was running his right hand over his bald head, wiping it almost, the gesture seemingly one he was both unaware of and helpless to avoid. "I hate big guys who think they own the goddam world," Osgood Percy said. "I should have just leveled him. Shit." He stopped dead, scowled at the dying moon.

D.D. waited, watching. He was still in his casino clothes, perfectly knotted tie, white shirt, dark jacket, dark slacks. If he didn't stop massaging his scalp she didn't know what she'd do, so she reached for his hands, took them, brought his manicured fingernails to her lips, held them there.

"In my line of work, it's best to be a gentleman, but sometimes it's very hard, Doris. There's an animal side to everybody."

"Oh, absolutely."

"One question—you don't think any less of me for walking out?"

"C'mon," D.D. said, starting to move toward their cars

again. "How can you even ask when I'm the one got you to go?"

"I ask because I think there's maybe some truth in it."

"You musta caught some kind of Saudi virus or something, 'cause you're not thinking straight."

"I'm *angry,* Doris—I have a terrible temper, I try not to let you see that side of me and you think I'm some kind of gentleman because that's what I want you to think, only part of me is very close to the jungle, do you believe—"

He stopped suddenly because behind them now there was a sound and when they turned the Mex was shoving the bar door open hard, moving a step into the night. He had boots on, and tight jeans, and a tapered shirt that clung to his body.

D.D. looked at Osgood Percy then, saw him blink; she was still holding on to his hands and she felt them start to tremble. "Help me in my car," she said.

"Yes, I will," he answered. "I'll do that very thing."

From behind them now, in the night, came the Mex: "Oh, Ozzie. Ozzie-Wozzie," repeated singsong.

They moved quickly toward their cars then, and D.D. got out her keys, unlocked the driver's side of her Chevette, waited as Osgood opened the door so she could slip inside.

During this, the "Ozzie-Wozzie" went on and on and—

—"Goddammit that's *enough*!" Osgood Percy said.

"Just tryin' for yer 'tension," the Mex said. He smiled and held out the wig with one hand. "I don' want this, Ozzie-Wozz—I wouldn't know what to feed it." He laughed for a while. "Come on—it's yours." He waved the wig in the darkness.

Osgood Percy looked at D.D., stared at her almost.

"Let's get outta here, okay?" D.D. said then.

Osgood Percy started toward the other man. Slowly.

"Osgood, for Chrissakes—" D.D. said.

"Oh, D.D.," the Mex called out, "we coulda had some times." Then he paused. "Maybe we will anyway—unless, of course, Ozzie-Wozzie here has any objections, you got any objections?"

Osgood Percy said nothing, just continued hesitantly moving toward the bigger man.

"Very businesslike type," the Mex said. "Not much interested in chitchat, that you, Ozzie?"

They were ten feet apart now. Osgood Percy stopped. Then he took another step forward, a smaller one. Eight feet. The Mex wiggled the wig. He made his voice high-pitched and smiled at D.D. as he said, "Good boy, 'at'sa good boy, Ozzie, come 'n' get it."

Five feet now.

D.D. sat behind the wheel, staring as Osgood Percy reached out with his right hand for his toupee. He inched closer, so that his hand was only a foot from it, then six inches, then the Mex went "Ooops" and the wig slipped from his fingers to the pavement.

Osgood Percy stared down at it. "Move away," he said then.

"Why?"

"Just move away."

"I will, once you tell me why, Ozzie."

"Safety precaution, let's say."

The Mex made a mock gasp. "You don't trust me? After all we been through together? You really think I might try tuh trick you?"

"Anything's possible," Osgood Percy said.

"Ozzie, I got a flash for you—*I don't need no tricks*!" And then he was staring off to where D.D. sat frozen behind the steering wheel and shouted, "D.D., you stay outta this an' get back in the car," and Osgood Percy turned then, turned his back on the Mex to look at her, and while his back was turned, D.D. cried out but there was no need.

Because the Mex did nothing. Just stood still smiling until Osgood Percy was watching him again. "See what I mean?" the Mex said again. "Who needs tricks for a peewee fag like you?" And before his words were finished he was moving toward Osgood Percy, swinging a giant roundhouse fist into Osgood Percy's face—

—D.D. stared, stunned, stunned and unbelieving, as Osgood Percy ducked and moved back a quick half step, then even more quickly he moved forward and dug a right hand into the Mex's stomach, sending the bigger man stumbling off balance, spinning toward D.D. where she sat in the car, and before the Mex could get set, Osgood Percy was on him, sending an explosion of pistonlike blows into the midsection of the bigger man, and now the Mex went down hard to the pavement, rolled over, holding his stomach, gasping.

Fists clenched, Osgood Percy moved toward the fallen drunk, close but not that close, moving from side to side slightly, always in perfect balance, waiting.

"Osgood?" D.D. said, when she was able to.

"Shut up," Osgood Percy told her.

"But—"

"—close—your—god—damned—mouth—Doris," Osgood Percy said then, in a tone she couldn't remember ever hearing from him. "No one's leaving 'til it's over." Now he pushed out at the Mex with his foot. "And it isn't 'til *you* say so."

The Mex moved into a sitting position, dazed, his voice soft. "Sorry," he said. "I go too far when I been drinking. I like t'have fun, only sometimes... sometimes, what I think's fun isn't fun for everybody. I'm real sorry. An' it's over." He reached out his right hand. "Help me up, okay?" and D.D. knew it was an act but Osgood Percy was such a sucker he didn't and before she could stop him he reached out, took the Mex's hand, helped him up—

—and then the Mex had him. Both his arms went around the smaller man's slim body in a giant bear hug and he raised Osgood Percy a foot off the ground and screamed, "Asshole, fucking asshole!" and in the air Osgood Percy turned his body left, turned it right, then slipped free of the giant's grip and began his attack. He buried a right into the Mex's stomach, and when the Mex lowered his hands to protect there, Osgood started a punch toward the face and the Mex got his hands up but no use, Osgood was attacking the middle again, and the Mex tried to move back and out of range but Osgood gave him no chance, and then as D.D. watched they were battling between the Chevette and the Rover and the Mex went down screaming and she got out of the car, standing there, listening to the rage just out of her sight no more than six feet away and should she run for the phone in the bar and call the cops or should she run around the car and try and cream the spick with her shoe or her purse or should she—

—she did neither, she did nothing, just stood where she was.

Frozen. Ashamed.

The Mex was screaming on and on, "I'll fucking kill you, you little prick," but then his cries became more quiet, as he said "kill" and then ". . . kill . . ." And then . . . Then the sound of more punches, but coming slower. Then a groan, a head hitting pavement. And following that, following that . . .

. . . silence.

No, not silence—she could hear the desperate breathing going on in the darkness—but no words.

"Osgood," D.D. whispered.

No reply.

"Osgood, you okay?"

D.D. wanted to run around and look then, but she was afraid, because what if she did that and Osgood was done and the Mex was waiting for her with his big hands?

"Osgood, come on."

But the Mex couldn't be waiting, not with the way Osgood was slaughtering him. Osgood was way too fast for him. Osgood had to be the winner.

So why wasn't he answering?

Now there was movement coming from the darkness on the other side of the Chevette. Movement and sound—coughing, the kind that rips the throat. And now hands were visible on the Chevette hood.

Big hands.

Big and red, bloody.

Aw, shit, D.D. thought. "Jesus, Osgood, it's me—"

"—I told you once already, Doris—close your goddamned mouth, you better learn to listen." And as he spoke, his voice flat, he stood shakily across from her. His face had some red on it. His shirt and tie had the dark spots too.

Now the big hands slid off the Chevette.

Osgood bent down, grabbed the hands, placed them back on the hood. Then he bent again, not so far this time, and as D.D. watched, the Mex began to appear, Osgood pulling him up by the hair.

After the hair came the face. Or what she could see of it—blood was pouring from his mouth, blood smeared his skin; his eyes blinked back blood. Osgood kept pulling and when the Mex was half up, he tossed him forward, the big body falling across the hood of the car.

Osgood Percy stood still a moment, getting his wind back. Then he reached out for the groggy big man, pulled him up off the car. "Okay—is it over? You tell me. Your call. I'm going noplace. I've got to tell you this—I hope you want more—believe that. I've loved these last few minutes. I could beat the shit out of you all night long."

The Mex blinked again, rubbed his hand across his eyes, trying to get the blood away. It still dripped from his mouth.

"I'd sure like an answer," Osgood Percy said, and he stepped back, got his fists ready for more.

Now, as D.D. stared, the Mex caved. A one-hundred-percent fold. He threw back his head and raised his hands, palms open and cried, *"Don' do nothin', please,* shit, lemme be!"

Quietly, Osgood asked, "Is it over, are we done?"

"Christ, lemme be, I don't want nothin' to do with you, I'm sorry, I'm sorry."

Osgood faked a right hand—

—the Mex screamed out loud, staggered back.

Osgood grabbed the other man then, pulled him upright—"That was a rotten thing I just did—scaring you—that was how an animal acts and I don't behave that way but I just did and do you know why?"

The Mex shook his head. "Nuh."

"Because *you*'re an animal and you brought that out in me—you bring people down to where *you* like it—"

The Mex just stared.

Osgood dropped his hands. "You don't understand what I'm talking about, do you?"

"Nuh."

Osgood Percy stepped back, rubbed his eyes. Then quietly he said, "I think you dropped something of mine."

The Mex kept on staring, wiping the blood from his forehead and eyes.

"My wig, please."

"Oh, yeah, right, sorry," the Mex said and he broke into a half run to where the toupee was, reached down, missed it, knelt, got it, then hurried back to Osgood. "Good as new, I didn't hurt nothin', see?" He held it out.

Osgood took it. "You didn't but you wanted to—you wanted to hurt me."

The Mex took a step back—"I didn't—not really—"

*"Don't you lie to me*—if you'd won, what would you have done?"

"Nothin'—Nothin'—I swear on my fuckin' sacred word of honor—"

Osgood made a fist again.

"Maybe I'd take your money."

"What about her?" Osgood thumbed toward D.D.

"Dunno."

"I do," Osgood Percy said. "You'd have robbed me and raped the woman I love."

There was a pause before the Mex said, "I wouldn't have hurt her, though."

Osgood Percy grabbed the Mex, shoved him hard against the Rover. The Mex brought his arms up protectively and said, "I don't want you to hit me no more. C'mon—din't I bring you the wig like you told me?—I'm really a good guy."

Osgood Percy glanced at D.D. "And this is what you were afraid of," he said. Then he turned to the Mex. "You know what you are? You're a coward and your breath is bad," and with that he gestured for the Mex to get the hell away and the Mex hesitated but not long. In a minute he was stumbling, getting his balance, then racing across the parking lot and around the corner and gone.

Osgood Percy stared after him, not moving.

D.D. hurried around the car, started to embrace him, stopped. The red on his jacket and shirt and tie was wet still, but that wasn't what stopped her. Rather it was his eyes. Was he racked about something? Why did he look sad when he should have been dancing? "You okay?"

No reaction. Then: nod.

D.D. hesitated, uncertain; then she took his hands. The skin was a little raw but there were no cuts. She brought the hands to her lips, made gentle contact. "Christ, what you did with these—" she began.

"—I don't want to talk about it."

"Not talk about it? How can you *not* talk about it, you zapped a fucking monster, Osgood, that's not the kind of thing you keep quiet about—I mean, shit, how many guys, gentlemen, like you, guys who dress nice and work with their minds, would even have the balls to take on a bastard that size, much less show him up the way you had him begging—"

"*He was drunk,* Doris—pissed out of his mind, if he hadn't been, he'd probably have cleaned my clock—"

"—bullshit, I know what I saw—"

"I don't want to talk about it anymore, goddammit, do you understand that?" He was staring at her now, and she didn't like the look.

"Don't get mad at me, huh, Osgood?"

He softened then. "I'm not mad at you. I just . . . this wasn't how I meant for the evening to go—we had important topics to discuss."

"I know that."

He started back toward the bar.

"Where you headed, Osgood?"

He pointed.

"Back in there? Not the way you're looking."

He blinked, glanced down at his clothes, registered the drying red smears. "Oh," he said. He fidgeted then, suddenly unsure which way was best.

"You ought to clean up. Maybe have some coffee. You don't seem in the best shape for discussing important topics."

"*But I am.*" He looked around, fidgeted some more.

"Maybe you better go to your place, change, clean up. I'll follow you." She pointed to their cars.

"Maybe," he said and went to his Rover, unlocked it, got in. She got into her Chevette, started the motor, waved to him and then followed his car to his place, a decent enough one-bedroom less than five minutes from Caesars. It was typical of him to live that near work—in case anything came up and they needed him, he could be right there. That was why he was going places—he was a company man all the way, you couldn't do better.

D.D. parked down the block because there was only

space for one car in his apartment area. He left the door open and when she got inside he was out of his bloody clothes and walking around in his underwear and socks with garters. She hated the garters, D.D. did, but not as much tonight as other times. "I'll run you a bath," she said, and did. When the tub was full she called him and he still had his underwear on but at least the garters were gone. "You soak," she told him. "You've earned it. Take as long as you want, I'll watch the TV."

She went to the living room then, turned on the tube. Not a hell of a lot to choose from, unless you liked test patterns. Fuck it, D.D. thought, because that wasn't what she wanted right then. She turned off the set, walked around the living room for a moment, then moved into the bedroom, ran her fingers up from her thick black belt, up the white sweater until they reached the tips of her bra, pressed in, gently pulled at what she could get of her nipples.

What she wanted right then was Osgood. Bad. It was the first time she'd ever known this intensity, at least for him. The husbands, all three, yes, at hitching time. But her drive for Osgood Percy began when he was battling out of her sight and the Mex was screaming and she could hear the punches and knew that she was the reason for the violence, the way she moved, her look, the power of the breasts she was touching now. The beginnings of her desire were what froze her by her side of the car, made her feel so ashamed.

She went to his dresser and rummaged around for his white silk pajamas. He only had the one pair that was silk, her gift, and nothing turned him on like seeing her walking around, strutting her stuff in just the top.

Now she put the white silk top on his neatly made bed, hesitated, picked it up, yanked the covers and blankets back, took two pillows, placed them in the middle of the mattress. Then, moving with silent purpose, she undressed, everything except for her bra. Carefully, she moved it down so that instead of cupping her, it was giving her additional support, making her jut out, something she'd only done once before for Osgood and he almost came unglued. Now she put the silk top on, buttoned it except for the highest two, sucked in her gut, took a look at herself in the mirror.

She was no kid, and sure, there were plenty who would think she was a top-heavy broad, but she had a way sometimes with some men, and as she pushed up on tiptoe, making her legs more slender, she knew now was going to be one of those times; there was no doubt whatsoever that the top of Osgood Percy's head was soon to come off. Just to make sure, she got the big candlestick from his dining area table, lit the candle with a match.

She walked to the half-open bathroom door, knocked. "I'm looking for a certain gentleman, one Rocky Balboa, the giant-killer, is he about?"

"Doris, I don't want to talk about it, I told you that already, now what is it?"

"My hair is turning grey with boredom, that's all."

"Well, I've been thinking—and anyway, you said I could soak as long as I wanted—"

"—I was younger then."

He sighed. "Okay, give me just a minute more, I've got to zero in on this Atlantic City thing—"

"—snooze."

*"What?"*

"I'm not interested in that particular subject just now, there's another topic that's more pressing, and it's this: shriveled skin."

"Huh?"

"I hate it, the way a person's skin gets all shriveled when they've been in the water too long." Now she snaked her arm inside the bathroom, found the wall switch, turned the place dark, entered by candlelight. "Stand up, Osgood."

He could not take his eyes off her.

She put the candlestick down on the sink, got a large

white towel, snapped her fingers. "Getting a little slow in your old age—out of the water like I told you."

He stood in the tub, reached a hand out for her.

"Not 'til you're dry," she said, and she took his arm, gently dabbed at it. "Other," she said.

He reached for her again.

"Don't get grabby, dammit."

"Listen—"

"—you got nothing to say that interests me, killer, now obey like a good boy." She dabbed at the other arm. "Okay, out. Out and turn around."

She could sense his breathing as she moved her hands along his back. "Turn."

He did, and then his hands were on her breasts.

"You want to touch my nipples with your tongue?"

"Yes."

"There's a condition."

"Anything you say."

"Burn your fucking wig."

He blinked, stepped away a moment, looked at her. "I thought you liked my wig. Or didn't mind it, anyway."

"I mind it, I hate it, I never want to see it again." She pushed his hands away from her body. "I didn't hear you say yes."

"It makes me look younger—it gives me confidence."

She handed him the towel, turned. "Dry yourself, if *I* don't give you confidence, we may as well pack it in."

He went after her, put his arms around her waist, moved his hands up over the silk top, gently began a circular motion.

"That supposed to turn me on? It doesn't—nothing turns me on except the word 'yes.' "

"Yes, all right, goddammit, okay, yes, I'll burn it. I'll invite the neighbors in if it makes you happy."

D.D. turned, took the towel back. She kissed him, ran her tongue in, then out, then began to dry his chest, slowly working her way down, his stomach, skirting his genitals, drying his thighs, then coming up with her fingers, touching him. He was hard, that didn't surprise her; what did was the size of him. Had he always been a stud? Maybe so, and it was like his blue eyes, something she chose not to dwell on. She knelt, dried his legs, and while she did she took him in her mouth for just a moment, felt him thrust forward, back, forward again.

She stood then, held on to his cock, led him slowly to the bed, lay down with her hips on the pillows, reached for him, gasped as he slid inside, began pumping his body. She locked her legs around him, closed her eyes tight, reached up and felt his firm body, found his nipples, squeezed them until they hardened. From far away now, she could hear the Mex screaming in the darkness of the parking lot and she lifted her hips for Osgood Percy, timing her moves to his. She brought an arm to her mouth, bit hard on her wrist to stay quiet, because she was going to be making a lot of noise in the not-too-distant future, she was already starting into a slow build toward orgasm, a wonderful gift from the shy strong man above her, her own private animal and who would have thought that an hour ago?

"When do we leave?" she managed.

He stopped, looked down at her.

"Keep *moving.*"

He rocked her again, his breath uneven too. "Atlantic . . . Cit-y?"

*"Yes."*

And then he shocked her. *"Why?"* he said.

D.D. hesitated, because she knew what he wanted to hear, and it wasn't the truth. The truth would have been "Why not?" or "I'll try anything once," or "How bad can it be?" except she couldn't say things like that, not to her balding mount who wanted so badly to hear the lie so she said it: "Love. Love you."

It wasn't a total lie. She did care. Some. And maybe it

would work out the way he wanted. The move. Then Love. Followed by Marriage. Anything was possible. And if it didn't take, well, maybe she wasn't good at arithmetic and, sure, her taste in men was subject to question, three strikes already, but to hell with that, fuck that, one thing she knew for sure, she gave great divorce.

# CHAPTER 3

# A Life in the Day of Nick Escalante

Mornings were never easy for him.

The way W. C. Fields felt toward Philadelphia was legendary, but Philly was Valhalla when compared to Nick Escalante's thoughts about Las Vegas, a city in which he was about to open his eyes for the five thousandth time.

So he fought his daily delaying action, wondering where he should visit, and as consciousness began to assert itself he went to Nepal, he hadn't visited Nepal in months, stupid of him if you knew what was waiting there—

—and he knew—how many times had he trekked alone along the narrow Himalayan trail, the views beyond the capture of camera, until he reached his destination, the village with the name that meant "hot water"—Tatopani. So special.

It was in the deepest gorge on earth.

On either side, close on either side, were wondrous peaks, peaks of legend, most notably Annapurna, twenty-three thousand feet above the gorge.

But you had to time it right. Yes, it was always worth the risks, starvation, frostbite, any of them. And yes, even if you started into the gorge at noon you would carry the memory.

But what about at twilight?

You race from the village into the darkening gorge, and then you turn, turn west, and there, still bathed in the yellow sun, is the whole of Annapurna, on fire to the top, and all for you. And you stand there in the cold of the gorge, you ignore the cold in the gorge, and you watch as the sun moves up the side of Annapurna, the yellow lessening in size, intensifying in depth. Where would you find a yellow like that again, ever, where in what country, continent, world?

Some died there, so the rumors said; they studied the yellow, committed it to as close to permanence as they were able, all the while forgetting the enemy of time, the enemy of cold. Some were found there, so the rumors said, found the next morning by old women out looking for firewood, the main fuel of the area.

But what if you lived through the twilight?

And you made it back to the village with the name that meant "hot water" and when you finally slept you knew that nothing could take away the yellow you had seen, you owned it, a spot to take your mind when the world grew wearisome; a spot like that, once you had it inside you, could banish discontent, or at the least, hold it at bay, or if not—

Nick Escalante shifted abruptly in bed, because he was beginning to lose his delaying action now; his concentration was getting weaker, and soon his eyelids would, involuntarily, flutter—

—or if not hold discontent at bay, then—

—then—

He began to force his mind now, desperate to get it back into the deepest gorge, and it shouldn't have been hard, because you could fly to Nepal from a lot of places now, Bangkok, Calcutta, Delhi, and once you landed you could drive close to where the Annapurna range began and then you could hike the rest, just move and keep moving and soon you'd be there, there where you so wanted, during twilight and—

—and—

—and his eyelids fluttered, opened; it was 10:00 A.M.—he needed no clock to tell him, he carried his own inside; it was always ten when he awoke, just as it was dawn before he could sleep. He had no way of knowing, of course, that a great deal of blood would be lost before he slept again.

Only some of it his.

He showered, shaved, dressed in the usual—tennis shoes, white gym socks, khakis, long-sleeved blue shirt—walked to his unbeloved bomb shelter of an office.

The week before Christmas. Vegas was dead. Not a show room open. This would all change, violently, come the 26th. But for now the desert wind held no promise of anything but cold.

Ten pieces of mail. Three junk, the other seven personal. He knew as he sat down and opened the first that none of the seven would be from a friend or an old girl who missed him. They would be, all, nut mail.

> Dear Mr. Escalante,
>
> Pardon me for intruding on your busy life and I wouldn't if it wasn't something that no one else could help me with and for years now, the fucking dog next door barks at me. Well, I can deal with that. Then, a month back, the bitch starts shitting on my front steps. I tell the owner to have his animal trained. He says I should blow it out.
>
> Okay, I call the cops. They say I should blow it out too, they got bigger fish to fry.
>
> WHERE HAVE THE RIGHTS OF THE CITIZEN GONE?
>
> I shoulda said this is a shepherd that is big and when it shits on

your front steps, it's a load. The owner thinks it's funny, but he won't when the dog is dead which is why I'm writing you—

Mr. Escalante, how do you garrote a dog? From the front or do you try and sneak up like it was human? I mean, do I say "Here, pootchy pootchy" and hold out a steak and when he starts to eat it, do I attack then?

This has become very important to me and I figured if anyone has the answers, it's got to be you so—

Escalante stared at the single-spaced pages, shook his head. How do you garrote a dog, dear God? He crumpled up the letter, pitched it toward the wastebasket, hit dead center, not such a big deal considering his entire office was less than twelve feet square and the basket was big.

Dear Nick Escalante—

I hope you're not insulted none by my using your name. (First name I mean. See above.) But I got a problem calling people "Mister." It's cost me a couple jobs already and here's the thing—I am, and I hope you don't think I'm bragging when I say this, one tough guy. Never backed away from a fight, no matter what.

Okay. I signed up with a buddy of mine to go down as a mercenary

> into someplace tropical, they won't tell us where yet because, you understand, they don't want security blown. The pay is good and I'm expert with firearms and all like that.
>
> My buddy, see, he's all gung ho about the two of us doing this together and I let on to him I'm gung ho too.
>
> Nick—I gotta tell somebody this—I'm squeamish. Jungles spook me—they have big black spiders and those little fish that can clean you to your skeleton in a minute—
>
> I can't back down, see, 'cause, as I said (see above) I never yet backed down, that's my rep and I gotta keep it.
>
> But I'm waking up nights now and all I have in my head is some memory of some python sucking me in. I'm the toughest guy I know, but the thing is, is it possible for tough guys to get afraid? Were you? Ever even once?

I'm scared *now,* Escalante thought, crumpling this paper, too, pitching it into the basket for another buzzer beater. Reading your letter is enough to scare anybody. Why not go garrote a shepherd dog and feel good about yourself?

He opened the next, got as far as the salutation "Sir," when the phone rang. Ordinarily, when it was this early, he'd let the machine answer, but the amount of nut mail—seven was way above his daily average—made him seek refuge.

An odd voice belonging to a Mr. Cyrus Kinnick announced itself in search of a Mr. Nick Escalante. Why odd? He closed his eyes a moment. Because it was assertive but soft, frail almost, in tone. Something odd in the accent too. Also the voice was young, surely under thirty-five, and no one named Cyrus should be allowed to be less than sixty.

Escalante said who he was, wondered who the hell the other man was, remembered that someone had written him weeks before about possibly using him toward the end of the month. He looked in his Monthly-Minder, which was totally empty except for the word "Kinnick" penciled in for the week before the holidays.

"May I be frank, Mr. Escalante?"

"And earnest. You can give a shot to 'aboveboard,' too, if you feel up to it."

"I'm not a humorous man, Mr. Escalante."

"Well, I think I just proved that I'm not, either, Mr. Kinnick. What do you want to be frank about?"

"You're not in the Yellow Pages."

Escalante said nothing, waited for a connective.

"I'm a cautious man."

Pronounced "caw-shus."

"When I arrive in a town I'm unfamiliar with, I try to assess the territory by thumbing through the Yellow Pages. The number of ads for female escort services did not come as a surprise, whereas the number of ads for churches did. And while I had the book in my hands, I thought I would look at your advertisement. Was it large? The largest? Was it boastful? I didn't know precisely what I was enquiring after but I did have curiosity. And I must tell you I was upset at not finding you there. I'm a considerable gambler, Mr. Escalante, if that isn't too boastful, and safety means much to me. I looked you up under every conceivable synonym for safety and there was no listing for you."

"You should have tried between 'chapels' and 'charm schools.' I don't want to be too boastful, either, Mr. Kinnick, but you are talking to the only 'chaperone' in all of Las Vegas, Nevada."

"That's how you refer to yourself?"

"I do, yes. I was told once that Robert Mitchum refers to himself as a 'starlet.' I decided if he could be a starlet, I could be a chaperone."

Now a pause. "I'm in a bit of a quandary," Cyrus Kinnick said finally. "When I wrote you from back in Boston—"

—pronounced "Bahs-ton" quite properly. What was improper was the lack of consistency in the accent—

"—I wrote on the recommendation of a business friend and neighbor who had used you and felt I might do the same. But when one gambles, the primary goal is, of course, winning, but after that, a secondary goal and for me always an important one is ambiance. Was the evening pleasurable? I'm not sure I find you very pleasurable, Mr. Escalante. I fear I may be too staid to enjoy your jocularity. Could you tell me a little something perhaps about yourself?"

"Wait a minute—you mean you want my qualifications?"

"Along those lines."

"Well, I've been knocked down, blown up, lied to, shit on and shot at, so nothing surprises me much anymore except the things people do to each other. I'm not a virgin except in my heart. I'm a licensed pilot, everything from Jennies through jets. I've taught karate in Tokyo and lectured on economics at Wharton. I can memorize the front page of *The New York Times* in five minutes and repeat it back to you in five weeks. I can follow anyone anywhere from in front or behind. I can go forty-eight hours without sleep or a drop in efficiency. I can bench-press four hundred and fifty pounds ten times without a break and was national Golden Gloves champion three years in a row. I speak four languages fluently and can wrestle with a menu in five more."

"Jesus—" from Cyrus Kinnick.

"*—and don't interrupt me,* I wasn't done, there's more!"

"More?"

"Yeah. I lie a lot."

And now from the other end of the phone, a surprising sound: an almost childlike giggle. "Was what you just told me all lies?"

"Not all."

"What wasn't true?"

"*The New York Times* takes ten minutes."

"Are you lying again?"

"Always."

"I'm at the Grand, Mr. Escalante. Stop by at nine tonight. Perhaps there's nothing all that wrong with jocularity. And perhaps I am too staid."

"Nine o'clock, Mr. Kinnick," Escalante said, and he hung up, studied the wall a moment. Ordinarily he would have never answered any question about qualifications. But Kinnick intrigued him enough to go along. Liars often intrigued him, at least at the start. He'd had a lot of clients over the years, Escalante had, but only one from Boston, and he had been dead a long while.

He flicked through the rest of the nut mail. The last letter almost broke his heart. It was written in pencil, the hand clearly shaky, and there was so salutation:

*I am sixty-two with a question.*
*Am I too old to be a great adventurer*
*like you? I never smoked or been drunk*
*and I weigh the same as always.*

*My wife died, just, so I figured what*
*the hell, take the chance.*
*But have I got one?*

*Is it too late for me to make it as a*
*man of action at my age?*

"It's too late for all of us," Nick Escalante said, getting the hell to his feet, because the clock in his head told him he'd been in his office for close to half an hour straight, and anything longer was bad for the system. Hazardous to the health. Sucked.

It did not take him many years to realize that there was no such thing as a good meal in Vegas. But like most old-timers (dear God, was he that? Yes. You couldn't argue with five thousand mornings), he came to know there was a best meal, and that was breakfast, because it was the one they could screw up least.

And the best breakfast in town was served at the coffee shop of the Silver Spoon Casino Hotel, just down the block from his office. More precisely at table seventy-five. His table. Reserved.

Roxy had been the day hostess at the coffee shop since the place opened twenty-some years earlier. She was the one who knew about table seventy-five. Escalante had done her something once and in return, the table became his. 11:30 on, just about every day.

Just as it didn't take him many years to learn about the food, the same was true about people's faces: If you lived in Vegas long enough, everyone began to resemble a movie or TV star. Roxy, for example, depending on your generation, was either Thelma Ritter or Rhea Perlman, the wonderfully funny brunet waitress on *Cheers*.

What made table seventy-five superior to all others was an architectural mishap. The ceiling of the Silver Spoon coffee shop was curved. And the acoustics were strange. If you sat at seventy-five, none of the adjacent tables was affected. But number fifty-eight, two tables away, was yours: even the slightest whisper from fifty-eight came booming happily to seventy-five.

It was his favorite spot in the town. His unofficial office. 11:30 'til 2:00 most days, then back for coffee around 4:00 'til whenever. Anybody who wanted to find him knew where he was.

Roxy gestured energetically toward him as he walked in. "You're missing Bible-Face, Nikki," she said, grabbing a menu, heading toward seventy-five. "I've had him at fifty-eight twenty minutes now."

Bible-Face was Roxy's name for the assistant room manager, a totally angelic-looking blond—try Ricky Schroder at thirty—and consistent churchgoer who probably scored as well as anyone in town. His post was near the front desk and whenever an attractive single woman signed in, Bible-Face saw to it that she was given room 899. Not only was it the worst in the hotel, he tipped a friend of his who worked as a janitor to see that the bathroom was under an almost continuous stage of siege—either the sink didn't turn on or wouldn't turn off and the toilet rarely flushed—and after a few minutes, Bible-Face would take the almost certain distress call coming from 899. He would go to the room himself, register dismay, escort the attractive victim to an enormous single, complete with mirrored ceiling and circular tub and insist she contact him if anything went wrong. And he would give her his card and he had a way of pressing her hand as he said good-bye that indicated he was someone you could count on if life ever got lonely.

Now, as he sat at table seventy-five, Escalante glanced around, saw Bible-Face sitting two tables away with a shockingly well-dressed woman of perhaps forty. Quite lovely. "...This is not a town for trusting people, Marie...," Bible-Face was whispering.

"What gambit's he using?" Roxy asked.

"The untrustworthy town," Escalante told her.

"She's dead but she won't lie down."

"Oh, she'll lie down; she just doesn't know how soon it's going to happen."

Roxy nodded, went off to get him his first cup of coffee.

"...I've told my share of untruths...," Bible-Face was saying now. "...When I first got to Vegas, I thought it was the way to quick success, since everyone else was doing it...."

"...You've got an honest face, Milton...."

"...That's why I was so good at it, Marie, and I'd be doing it still except for the churning up I did inside...."

"...You mean your conscience...?"

"...You see how quickly you picked up on that? Oh, God...."

Escalante sat at his table, carefully not studying the torment at table fifty-eight. It was his memory that the "special specimen" move was at present under way.

"...I married when I was very young, Marie.... I'm not wearing a band, you wouldn't have known except I *want* you to know.... It's been a dreadful marriage, just rotten...."

"...You mean joyless...?" Marie asked.

"...Oh, God...you picked right up on that too...," Bible-Face said, staring sadly down at the tabletop. "...I can't leave her because of the kids...and I don't mind it so much except sometimes...like when fate, through a toilet that won't flush, brings me in contact with a special specimen like you...a sensitivity like you have makes me know what my life might have been....You're leaving today, you're going back to your travel-agency job and all the glamour it entails....I'm here, with a wife who hates our beloved children and..."

Roxy was returning now with the coffee; Escalante put his finger up for quiet. Roxy sat alongside.

Bible-Face stared into the lovely woman's eyes now, reached out, took her hands. "...I can get a key to a suite that rents for a thousand dollars, Marie...with a view of all Las Vegas sweeping outside....You're free forever, but I'm only free 'til one o'clock. Beloved, give me something to remember...."

There was a long pause until she nodded. Bible-Face stood, glanced toward Roxy. "On my tab, Rocks?"

"You got it, Milt."

The ex-inhabitants of table fifty-eight moved out of the coffee shop, bodies close.

"He's not so good-looking, I don't get it," Roxy said, standing, getting ready to head back to her station by the door. "I really do not get it."

"He wants it that much," Escalante said.

Roxy shrugged, started away.

Escalante sipped his black coffee, wondered what country he should head for. There was a glacier in New Zealand where you could ski for eighteen miles, eighteen consecutive miles, incredible—

—no—he'd been to the Himalayas already today and it was chilly outside—

—that island in the Canaries—Lanzarote—that was the place—sixty miles off the African coast—that was a special place, Lanzarote—and not just because of the landscape with its lava craters—

—it was the black-sand beaches stretching out that beckoned to him—

—he had never walked a black-sand beach.

There was a fancy hotel on the island now. He read whatever he could about travel and when he learned that the hotel was going to scar Lanzarote he was ticked for a while, because he knew about the place before there was any thought of fancy building. But he dealt with the bad news, because crowds never were the kind of thing you should let deter you, crowds could be beaten, and the way the black beach could be yours was simple, sleep there, alone, with the pale blue water just starting to lap the dark sand.

Escalante stared at his coffee, thinking that if scoring was what Bible-Face wanted that much, well, he had his "that much," too, and it was this: just to keep moving. Never put your head down on the same pillow twice.

If he had a god it was motion.

There was nothing he didn't want to see. He knew the best way to reach the lost city of the Incas, and the climb through the clouds to get there was an ascent he'd read about and studied. And in New York he had memorized the order of the main gallery in the Frick Collection, where the Turners were, the Rembrandts, the Corots, and the hours he knew, too, ten to six, Tuesday through Saturday, one to six Sunday, don't go Monday, closed Monday, and this, the greatest of all small museums, cost exactly a buck, and after the Frick, one of the things you could do in New York that was special was take the hike to the papaya place on East Eighty-sixth Street for the best hot dog in the city, and it was cheap, too, but travel wasn't, not if you wanted to experience it all, a barge in the autumn through Burgundy, he had that brochure stuffed back in his room in some cardboard box or other.

Twenty thousand dollars.

That was what he needed. Per year. Except one year was next to worthless, after one year you'd just be getting warmed up, you'd barely have begun to forget your five thousand mornings after only one year.

He needed, no question, a hundred thousand dollars. Exactly that. For five years of freedom. His total worth as he sat in the Silver Spoon was—putting as realistic a value as he could on everything—probably closing in on the three-hundred-dollar mark.

But then, November had been a bad month. And the first week in December hadn't been a whole lot better. But the best thing about luck was that it changed. Everyone else's did. His would.

He'd get his hundred thousand cash. No question. But the worst thing about luck was that it never lingered. Sometime, soon probably, the opportunity would be there—*there*—ready for the plucking.

He just had to be good and damn sure *he* was ready too. He would be. He knew that. What he had no way of knowing was that the hundred thousand would be in his hands in less than fifteen hours as he sat in the Silver Spoon, watching as Osgood Percy came steaming in through the coffee-shop doorway.

"It worked, it fucking worked," Osgood Percy said, taking the seat across from Escalante, running his right hand across his bald head where the wig usually was.

Escalante stared at him. "How could you be such a bastard, Oz, saying what you said to me like that?"

"Huh?"

"You told me I was a coward and my breath was bad—that's not an insult, that's overkill."

"It just popped out in the heat of battle—and speaking of being a bastard, why didn't you tell me your mouth was going to start bleeding like that—I was scared I'd screwed up everything."

"Just trying to keep you on your toes."

Osgood Percy got out his wallet. "Fresh from the bank." He counted out five hundred-dollar bills, put them on the tabletop.

Escalante stared at the money. "That's not the right amount."

Osgood Percy took a moment before replying, "I'm not a crook."

"Nobody said you were."

"I'm not a crook and I'm very good with numbers so yes, that is the proper amount and I'm going to prove it, because this began what, two days ago, when I came to you and I said, 'Would it be all right if I beat the shit out of you?' and you were intrigued, asked why and I explained I had a girl friend that wasn't all that anxious to come to Atlantic City with me because I suspected, deep down, she thought I was a nerd, and if she could just see me as a man of action, bringing down a big guy, showing her what I'm made of, I just knew it'd change her mind. Right so far?"

Escalante nodded.

"Then you said okay, you'd never done anything close to that, it might make for an interesting change, and you set up the place and me coming half an hour late and all the rest and we talked price: hundred fifty for your time and trouble, a second hundred fifty if she came to Atlantic City, that's three. And I said about the bonus. I said if she just came along out of boredom or because of all the pressure I was putting on, that was it, but if I was right, if what I knew deep down—that she loved me, really all-the-way *loved* me—was true, and if she'd come out and say that, if me beating the shit out of you could bring that out, make her see the real me, then there'd be a two-hundred-dollar bonus that would bring the total up to five."

"And that happened?"

"Oh, shit, just like I knew it would. I said, after she'd said she'd come along with me, I said, 'Why?' and she was surprised but she admitted the truth: She fucking loves me!"

Escalante sat staring down at the bills, remembering the flustered woman with the white sweater tucked in tight and the way she looked up at him and muttered "Manilow" and how she spoke too much to him, telling him more than she needed. "I'll take the three hundred," Nick Escalante said.

His breakfast always began like something out of *Five Easy Pieces.* He liked to start with fresh grapefruit juice and all the hotels in Vegas, of course, had that on their menus, except what they meant by "fresh" was "frozen."

So what he had done for years now was begin with two grapefruit halves and a large glass of ice. He'd become quite adept at squeezing the fruit into the glass without waste, and of course it was expensive and it also took a lot of stirring before the juice got cold enough, but you had to take your triumphs where you found them, however small.

He was stirring the juice, sipping on his second cup of coffee, when the call came. Roxy gestured to him from up near the cashier, holding the receiver in the air. He nodded, stood, walked over. "It's a Miss Helen Hollister," Roxy said.

Escalante looked at her a moment, then took the phone. "Miss Hollister?"

The voice was controlled. "Correct. I'm in town staying at a girl friend's who's on vacation. Chestnut Street, 1108 Chestnut Street, it's downtown, off Fremont. I was hoping you could come visit. In the very near future. If such a thing is possible."

"'Such a thing' would only be possible if you'd answer a question."

"Speak."

"Why the 'Miss Hollister' bullshit, Holly?"

"Because I wanted . . ."

He listened as she took a breath. The control was going. She was in pain. Escalante knew about that.

". . . because it was important . . . important to me that you not act out of . . . an unprofessional concern. . . . I need you, Nikki, can you come . . . ?"

"In the very near future."

"Have you had your grapefruit juice yet? If you haven't, don't waste it."

Escalante hung up, shaking his head; he'd known her since she was fourteen and she had been mothering people then.

It was quarter of one when he parked his rented Ford in front of 1108 Chestnut. Everything Escalante had was rented—apartment, office, car. He even had a storage space rented out near Mojave Road, a twenty-four-hour open spot where he could lock whatever he wanted, travel stuff mostly, the books and magazines collected over the years; when he had his hundred thousand, when that cash was warming his hands, he would be gone within an hour, he had his departure totally planned; it had been for years.

He rang the 1108 bell, heard her "Unlocked," walked inside. Dark. Small house, two bedrooms. "I made you coffee in the kitchen," her voice called out from behind a bedroom door. He found the coffee, poured himself a cup, walked back into the living room. "Okay?" Her voice still came from behind the bedroom door.

"Tastes fine."

"Should. A hundred percent Colombian."

"Holly, if you're going to hide, why couldn't we have just talked on the phone?"

"I don't think I want you seeing me."

"Oh, shit, is this a Joan Crawford picture?"

Now a long pause. Then the door opened. She came in slowly, but even in the dark he could see the half-closed eyes, the swollen mouth, the broken nose. She moved in a disjointed way. She was wearing a cloth robe. Probably more of her was broken under the material.

It was important that he sip on his coffee, so he did.

"Hey, Mex," Holly said.

He nodded.

"I called out for you in Emergency. One of the doctors said so. I guess I kept saying 'Mex' over and over. They figured you were the one who..."

He watched her in the pause. Of all of them, she had been the toughest. The gold-star girl. The optimist who wouldn't allow the existence of an all-black night, but now he thought she couldn't help it, she had to cave. "...who violetted me..." she said finally.

She was still the toughest, coming out with that joke just then. When he'd first met her she'd been to a movie and when he asked what it was about she explained it was about a nice girl and a nasty man who had his way with her. "'Had his way'?" Escalante had asked. "Yeah," the fourteen-year-old had answered. "Y'know—violetted her."

"Last night this happened?"

"Start to finish."

"Go."

They moved to the couch, sat at opposite ends. He sipped his coffee, watching as she tried to get comfortable. After a little she gave up in the attempt. "I had a date last night. Nice guy. We had a nice time, blah-dee-blah. No shows to see but we ate at the good place in Caesars and hit the tables after that and went to a couple other hotels, blah-dee-blah, until he was tired. Did I say he was an old guy?"

Escalante shook his head.

"Well, you could see him starting to conk out, he made dumb bets, and he'd been drinking and when he was losing a lot I said why don't we bag it, best to bag it when the tables get mean, and I think he wanted *me* to think he was a swinger but you could see the relief when I said to end things and I went up to his room, had a nightcap, blah-dee-blah, and pretty soon I was back in the hall, waiting for the elevator, and it came, and the doors opened, only this was the up elevator and there were some people inside, three, but really only one."

"Again?"

"The one was the boss, you could tell that, the big guys were flunkies and the boss—he was built powerful, like Stallone—he thought he was *it*, you could tell right off he wasn't into inferiority and he said 'C'mon to the party' and I said thanks but no and he said 'Hey, I'm too pretty to turn down' and with that he pulled me into the elevator and smiled his wop smile and I figured 'Easy, don't make a scene,' they didn't seem drunk or like that and I been in situations before, blah-dee-blah." She paused, looked down at her hands. "I think maybe some coffee would do me too," she said, started to try and stand.

"I need a refill anyway," Escalante said, and he went to the kitchen, came back with two cups now, handed one over.

She took it, nodded, was quiet until she said, "Where was I?"

"'Blah-dee-blah,'" Escalante told her.

It brought a smile.

"The elevator went up, I didn't look to see the floor, I had other things on my mind, like how best to make my departure when the opportunity presented, and then we were in Stallone's suite. Just the four of us and I said 'Where's the party?' and he said 'You're it' and I didn't like that a whole lot, and then he asked how I felt about champagne and I said I wasn't interested in drinking and he said 'Hey, this is Dom Pérignon,' and he said it like I was supposed to swoon or something except the shithead pronounced it like this: 'Dome Pear—igg-non' and what I wanted was just to break out laughing but like I said, I been in situations before so I made like 'Wow, all my life I've been waiting for a fucking sip of good old Dome Pear-igg-non'—I had to say it that way, too, right? right, and he snapped his fingers and one of the big blond guys went scurrying over to this fridge and got out a bottle and while he was opening it, Stallone excuses himself and goes into the bedroom and I'm in the living room with the two big mothers and there was no question I wasn't going anywhere, so I stand at the window and stare out at the Strip and figure my best move, which I decide is, first chance I get, start in on a good sob story, because I know, I can just feel, that within maybe half an hour, Stallone's going to make a pass at me and he didn't seem like the kind who liked rejection.

"Then I hear his voice going 'I just hadda get comfortable' and I turn and I think 'Holly, it's not going to be any half an hour' because he's got his socks on and he's taken off his clothes and put on a robe—except it's untied, and it's open down the front. Then he says to the big guys that there must be something they'll like on the tube and they head into the bedroom and he pours a couple glasses of champagne and ambles over to where I am and he says 'Oh, you are one special bitch' and I said 'Am I ever, Dome Pear-igg-non' and he says 'No, that's not it, what makes you special is you're the only broad in all the world tonight that gets to touch it' and I go for ignorance, bat my eyes and ask 'Touch what?' and he just smiles and looks down at himself and says 'The Envy of All Mankind' and right now I am, for the first time, very scared because when a guy has a name for his cock, you know he's not playing with a full deck." She sat silently then.

Escalante waited.

"I tried cooling things, but nothing I tried worked. You don't want to hear any more."

"I didn't want to hear this much."

Holly made a nod. "It all gets fuzzy along about here anyway."

Escalante nodded back, wondering why she had decided now to start lying.

"I guess he did what he did and then the big guys beat up on me and then I was dumped in the service stairs and then the emergency ward. Blah-dee-blah."

Escalante nodded again, waited.

She pulled a bill out then from a pocket in her robe. "Isn't fifty what you charge the first hour?"

"This is my day for turning down money. What do you want to pay me for?"

"I want to sue the son of a bitch, Nikki."

Another lie. "Then you must hire a lawyer, Holly; I'm not a lawyer, I would make a terrible lawyer."

"I don't know his name or any goddam thing about him—I don't know what he's called or what room he was in or where he's from or squat."

"Then you must hire a detective, Holly; I'm not a detective, I would make a worse detective."

"I don't know any goddam detectives!—I know you and you know everybody."

"I can give you the names of several competent men."

"Why are you *doing* this, Nikki? How can you not help me?"

"Every so often I try and remember the existence of logic. Logic tells me that the three gentlemen you told me about were not, I'm really sure of this, were definitely not executives of either IBM or Chase Manhattan. What hotel were you in?"

"The Croesus."

"Better and better."

"A lot of people like it."

"That's true. And so is this: Every high school student in America knows there is no such thing as organized crime in this country. And every grammar school student knows that if organized crime ever dreamt of staking a toehold in this great land of ours, the last place it would try would be here in our wondrous fairyland of Las Vegas. And every goddam kindergarten kid knows that if organized crime ever did get started here, the last hotel in the world to become tainted would be The Croesus. Shit, Holly, even their chorus girls can rip the phone book in half."

"You're gonna help me, I can tell—when you go on a tear like this, it means you're coming around."

He stood suddenly, put the coffee cup back in the kitchen, returned. She was seated as before.

"I appreciate everything you're gonna do for me, Nikki."

"You always could piss me off."

"I know."

He sat beside her. "I'm leaving now and I want everything clear: Holly, when I came to this town and you were just the little kid with pimples who lived across the street—"

"—you go to hell, I always had a good skin—"

"—that first year the Combination tried to hire me. Baby himself. He didn't run things then but we talked and I said 'No, if someone got bloody, I wanted it to be for my reasons and not anyone else's.' Baby accepted that. And since then, I have stayed away from them and they have stayed away from me. I don't know anything about the Combination, Holly, and on my word of honor, I don't know a soul who works The Croesus, I don't have one contact there, I swear to God."

"I can always tell when you're lying and you're lying now!"

He was; they could always read each other so well. Probably that was the saddest reason it never worked out. Or one of the saddest.

"Just find out who he is so I can sue and put his ass in jail. I'll be here all day waiting for your call."

"Don't wait, I'm not calling."

"My Mex, he always comes through," Holly said.

It was the conviction with which she said it that sent him out into the afternoon, furious. He got into his car, gunned away, hit the brakes a few blocks later at the first pay phone he came to, got out, dialed The Croesus, asked for housekeeping, decided when they answered to try black.

"Housekeeping."

"Gimme Millicent, this be Godfrey." Millicent weighed 290, which was fine for Wilt Chamberlain but didn't do much if you stood five three. Still, men were always after her, so her mood was usually sunny. She'd gone through a bad time a few years back but Escalante had done her something then to ease her way.

"Which Godfrey?" Millicent said when she came to the phone.

"Me."

Her voice dropped. "They don't like us getting called a whole lot."

"Then I'll be quick—see if you can get anything on a guy looks like Stallone who has a suite somewhere, I'd guess the top floors, and he travels with two very large blond gentlemen. Bodyguards."

Pause. "You still live in Naked City?"

"I do."

"You know where the nigger McDonald's is?"

"Of course—the best bouillabaisse in town."

"Huh?"

"Nothing; yes, I know where the nigger McDonald's is."

"Okay. I get off at four. You be there at four-fifteen. If I'm not there, I couldn't find nothing; if I am, we'll talk."

"One last thing," Escalante said.

"Be quick."

"How'll I recognize you?" He hung up to the sound of her laughter, dialed Pinky, who had the office next to his and his key, so that when he couldn't face it, he could have Pinky check to see if there were any messages on his machine.

"Lima to Rio," Pinky said when he answered, kind of their game. Whenever Pinky found out the air time between what he considered oddball cities, he'd spring them, hoping to trip up the Mex, something he'd never done.

"Four hours fifty," Escalante said when Pinky picked up again a couple of minutes later.

"Shit," Pinky said, and then, "Well, there's two and they both sound like nut cases. The first was from someone named Kinnick who said for you to be sure to be armed." He paused. "Does that mean a gun, Nikki? Hell, do you even own one?"

"What kind of an insulting question is that to someone in my profession? You're goddam right I own a gun." It was true. The size of a Magnum. Deadly grey. It was also made of wood and had been whittled for him by a client years before out of some kind of lunatic gratitude. "What's the second?"

"No name, strained voice, four words: 'The Reverend says please.' Make sense?"

"Alas," Nick Escalante said.

There are certain books, works of nonfiction generally, that achieve an impact and fame far beyond their sales figures. Nader's *Unsafe at Any Speed* for one. Friedan's *Feminine Mystique* was another. And in 1978, *Owning God* by Darryl Paxton.

It was an expertly researched and detailed attack on the sincerity and finances of the dozen leading television preachers—Roberts, Swaggart, Falwell, Humbard, etc. The book was written in a dry style, devoid of hyperbole, and the publicity firestorm it generated was entirely attributable to one simple fact: Darryl Paxton, the Reverend Darryl Paxton, had been, up until 1976, as successful a television preacher as any of the men examined.

In '76 the revelation struck that he had wandered far from the fields of the Lord, and in remorse and despair, he gave up his renown and wrote *Owning God*. In fact, if he was particularly harsh on anyone in the book, it was the chapter that dealt with his own fall from grace. He spared himself not at all, ripped his motives mercilessly, detailed his seduction and religious hypocrisy. If there was a villain to the book, it was the author. If there was a heroine, it was his wife, Ashley, whose mother had been reading *Gone with the Wind* while pregnant and very much wanted a son.

Escalante, when he met them, was soon to realize that while Darryl was impossibly unfair to himself, he was, if anything underrating Ashley. She was that special.

When he did meet them, in '78, it was not of his own choosing. They were famous in the town—part of Darryl's TV "spiel" was that he intentionally attacked the Devil in his stronghold, Vegas: Darryl had headed perhaps the biggest and richest Baptist church. Then in '76 he resigned and they disappeared from attention until the publication of the book.

One of their greatest admirers was Chief of Detectives Galloway in town, and he was the one who called Escalante in. They, the Paxtons, were receiving threats on their lives and needed protection for their book tour.

"Book tour?" Escalante said. "Sounds deeply religious, if you ask me."

"The money goes to charity," Galloway said. "They're both rich anyway, big rich, inheritances. And I want them safe while they're out of town. They're doing the Donahue show in Chicago and several of their threats have been mailed from there. You're on the case—bring 'em back alive, Frank Buck."

"Why me?"

"'Cause he wants you—I gave him a bunch of names, yours was the one he jumped at—he's a Christian minister, maybe he's got a soft spot in his heart for ethnics."

"And if I say no?"

"Then I'll get on *your* case, Mr. Mexican smart-ass. I don't think you want every cop in this town hassling you for the rest of your life, do you?"

Bring on them Christians, was all Escalante could reply.

Darryl Paxton was a Spencer Tracy type. Grey-haired, mid-forties, chunky, he had a firm handshake and always looked people in the eye. There was the unmistakable air of sincerity in everything he said. Sincerity, decency, honesty, goodness.

Escalante found him almost totally repellent.

"It's keen of you helping us along, Mr. Escalante."

(He also said "keen.")

"I can't imagine escorting a couple of codgers like Ashley and myself is your idea of heaven."

(Along with "codgers.")

"One thing I'd like to get set: I don't have any fear anymore. You ever get a message from me that says 'The Reverend says please' you'll know I'm afraid. But your job is Ashley. Anyone wants to do me bodily harm, well, either I can take care of myself or The Good Lord didn't want me to."

(Not to mention "The Good Lord.")

They were standing on the front steps of the Paxton house, which didn't seem particularly unusually large, but it was three houses down from Wayne Newton so Chief of Detectives Galloway's remark that they were rich was probably true. "Ashley's in the back," Paxton said. "Let's mosey out and meet her."

(*Nobody* said "mosey.")

If Darryl was Spencer Tracy in appearance, Ashley Paxton was a long way from Hepburn. To draw her, you'd simply make circles and put one on top of the other. She was overweight, yes, but not that fat. She was just very short, five one, and everything about her, head shape, arms, even fingers, was round.

The three of them chatted for fifteen minutes and probably it took all of a third of that time before Escalante realized that the balloon lady was an unusual creature. Her smile was quick and natural, and that was part of it. But not as large a part as her tranquillity. And both of these were less important than her eyes. Not the color, a deep enough blue. Not the size, although they were, undeniably, large. There was something more, an understanding shining from somewhere inside, and as he watched her Escalante hoped he never had any government secrets, because he realized that if he did, and her eyes were turned enquiringly on him, he would be helpless.

They took the 1:00 flight to Chicago the next afternoon for the television appearance. (It would turn out to be a quiet trip, except for the one phone call. Just after the Donahue show had ended, someone had gotten on the line, asked for Ashley, and when she'd answered, very quickly said enough to cause her to become hysterical. Darryl rescued her, held her 'til her tears dried, "There-there'd" her back to her natural tranquil state. Escalante wondered if there was something he might do. Darryl shook his head, said the only proper thing anyone could do with deranged people was ignore them.)

Within ten minutes of the 1:00 to Chicago's departure, Darryl Paxton was asleep. Ashley turned to Escalante. "He works so hard, it always pleases me when he can rest."

Escalante nodded.

"This book has taken so much out of him—we get so many threats now—you see, people think we've betrayed the church and some even see Darryl as evil. The Devil has won him over. But I know no Devil is strong enough for my man."

"He seems just like a keen human being."

Long pause. Then: "Was there some sarcasm involved in that, I wonder?"

"I'm never sarcastic when clients are involved, Mrs. Paxton."

"You don't like Darryl very much, do you?"

"I never make personal judgments when clients are involved, Mrs. Paxton."

She glanced out the window. "I do believe a lightning bolt is headed in your direction."

Escalante said nothing.

"I know why."

"Why?"

"It's because Darryl's just so *good* it sets your teeth on edge, isn't that true? Your jaws ache, admit it."

"You seem like a fine and perceptive woman, so may I suggest that you use your perception to see that this line of conversation is not going to do anyone any benefit."

"Admit it!"

"All right—your husband *is* tough to take—I mean, it's not just the way he talks, it's more that perfection in human form is always a little hard on the rest of us. And if he's perfect, and you're his helpmate, I have to assume some of it has rubbed off on you."

"I've got a wicked tongue, beware."

"I'm sure."

"You are an arrogant shit, Mr. Escalante, and I'm tempted to say it right out loud but of course, being perfect, I never would."

Escalante began to laugh.

Now she was laughing too—"Shall we have a double Scotch and get to know each other?"

He nodded and they did and it was during their second double that the subject of the interview came up, the one that made him, in a very small way, celebrated.

"I feel very safe, with you and all," Ashley said. "I wasn't worried for myself, but when the threats over the book began, Darryl took to fretting over my safety. That's when he consulted Detective Galloway." She paused. "Are you really so dangerous?"

"Oh, come on."

"Galloway said you were."

"I can't help that."

"He read about you, he said."

"I can't help that either."

"You helped write a book; I'm surrounded by authors."

Escalante sipped his Scotch.

"What was it called? He told me, I've forgotten."

"I didn't write a word."

"But you talked to the author."

"To my eternal regret."

"Then why did you do it?"

Escalante shrugged. "Dumb. And I found myself in a situation with a lot of time to waste."

"It said you were blown up and recuperating in a hospital." She opened her purse, took out some photocopies of magazine pages. "Detective Galloway gave this to me." Now her eyes were on him. "I'd like to hear it from you."

Escalante took a long pull at his Scotch. "I was an M.P. Saigon. This officer came to me. Said he'd heard about me. He was writing a book, he'd written others but this was to be his last: *Our Friend Violence.*"

"That's the title I couldn't think of—creepy, if you ask me."

"I'm with you. I told the guy—Captain Dan MacShane—'No.' He was famous but I didn't know it—there's a whole weird subculture out there where names like Fairbairn of Shanghai rank with Jesus—Fairbairn invented what he called The Timetable of Death. Like I said, a very bizarre group lies around trying to be like Fairbairn or Captain Dan MacShane. Anyway, he came to see me when I was in the hospital and he said since I had nothing else to do could he ask me some questions and I said 'Okay, just don't let on where you got the answers' and for weeks and weeks he'd visit and ask and I'd talk and he'd take notes and then, I guess back in '68, the book came out and became, in that world, a classic, like *Cold Steel* or *Kill or Get Killed.* I didn't even know it was published or care. Then, ten years ago, MacShane did his interview."

She waved the photocopied pages. "This?"

He nodded. "It was done originally in a magazine for mercenaries but it got reprinted a lot, every year or so, in self-defense periodicals, the kind of stuff people who dream of being soldiers of fortune get off on. MacShane was talking about his book and he said he had to get something off his chest, because he was a sick man and he didn't want to pack it in with this on his conscience. But two of the chapters were basically not his."

Ashley licked her finger, turned a page. "'Give In to Win' and 'Everyday Death.'"

Escalante nodded.

"Why is this so terrible?" Ashley asked, and began to read softly. "'These chapters are really the words of a young man named Nick Escalante. I think they are strong and true but I don't feel the credit should be mine. Nick lives in Las Vegas now, where he specializes in personal security work. His reputation with the military police, before he got hurt, was exemplary and I would say without question that, in a situation that did not involve firearms, from twenty feet on in he is the most lethal man alive.'" She stopped. "That's not exactly bad publicity."

"No, it's been great. I get letters every day from crazies, asking how would I go about killing this person or that beast. I get phone calls from Young Turks who beg to go against me to the death—true—there hasn't been a major mercenary convention or war weekend that I haven't been asked to give a speech at—*and I hate it all, Ashley.* All the right-wing, let's-stock-up-on-ammo survivalists who can't wait to blast the shit out of all the commies in Grenada so they can save the world by blowing it away and they will not ever leave me the hell alone."

"You're not a violent man, then?"

"I'm just good at it," Nick Escalante said.

It was going on two when he pulled up in front of the Paxton house. Wayne Newton had moved in the six years that had passed since Escalante first met them, but the neighborhood had managed to sustain the blow. Real estate prices had gone up, for whatever reason.

A lot had changed since their meeting. A friendship had developed; that was good. The Paxtons had opened The Knot—named for the old expression about what do you do when you come to the end of your rope?—you tie a knot and hang on. The Knot was in one of the worst parts of Vegas, and was free, entirely supported by the Paxtons' money. Anyone could go to The Knot for a clean bed and plain food—tapped out compulsives, drunks who weren't ready to accept the blessings of A.A.—but in the main, the place was used by teenagers, kids who'd come to town seeking whatever, hadn't found it, had begun sliding down at the always increasing speed; a lot of suicides had been prevented by The Knot; it was a major change and no one doubted that it was good.

The only bad changes had happened to Ashley, but you wouldn't have heard it from her. But it was as if she were working her way through seven years of afflictions. A hip shattered on a wet bathroom floor, arthritis, the ordinary kind, then rheumatoid, so that her hands were misshapen, the pain constant. Then, two years before, when she was forty-eight, the problem with her eyelids.

Technically, the condition was known as blepharospasm, and it wasn't all that uncommon, thousands of people a year get it, perhaps more. What happens is that for reasons yet undetermined, some think a tiny stroke in the brain stem, the eyelids lock. Involuntarily. Without warning. And they stay locked sometimes for seconds, sometimes minutes, and even pulling cannot halt the spasm. The lids stay locked until, no one knows why or when, they choose to relax. Because of the total unpredictability of it all, most victims become functionally blind. Even though they can see perfectly. Ashley had been functionally blind for going on two years, and even though there was a possibility of surgical aid, she chose to avoid it, since even if it worked, it left part of the face in a state of paralysis.

Ashley did her best to cope. She was, of course, in many

ways, helpless, couldn't drive, couldn't be trusted where any kind of movement pertained, since the locking might happen anytime, and if she was trying to walk across a street, danger or chaos or death were all reasonable results. She was simply not to be trusted much alone and Darryl left her rarely. Which was, all in all, not such a hardship for him. They had always been joined at the hip.

The one element that didn't change was Darryl. He still kept his calm Spencer Tracy face to the world, "moseyed" here and there, took Ashley's troubles better than possible, considering the depth of his caring.

The lack of change was one of the reasons Escalante was so surprised as the door to the Paxtons' house opened before he could knock and Darryl, drained and calm no more, beckoned for him to enter quietly. "I don't want Ashley to know," Darryl whispered. "She's napping now." He gestured and Escalante followed him into the library. Darryl closed the door.

"Know what?" Escalante said then.

"A note arrived. From Los Angeles." He pointed to the desk. "I read it and called you. It's a kidnap note, Nicholas—and we have no children."

Even for what it was, it was vile. Escalante read it over several times, careful not to touch it. It was done in standard fashion—individual letters and words cut from newspapers and magazines, all glued to an oversized piece of brown paper.

DEar God loveR
DeAR PricK GOD LoveR BASTARD
COCK
YOUR TimE IS OVER at LAST—
vengEANCE IS Mine!
EvEN a Phony CoCk PRICK
GOD LOVER
SHOULD know WhO SaID
That.
you WANT to SEE your
BABY blue Dumpling
AGAIN?
you want HER saFe and CUDDLED
in YOUR PHony ARms
AGAIN?
BET you DO.
WONdER IF YOU WILL.

"What do you think I should do?" Darryl said, hovering by Escalante.

"Nothing—it's a nut note. You said it was from L.A., didn't you? That explains everything. Anyway, there are no instructions *for* you to do anything. I think it's just something meant to scare you. Probably this guy writes them for a hobby."

"Doing nothing feels wrong, Nicholas."

"Then go to the cops. They know you. Hell, they even like you."

"I don't think I want to do that. I was going to call them before I called you. But then . . . I was afraid they would have to ask questions, and not just of me."

"You're right, they would, and Ashley's got enough troubles going just now, if that's what you mean."

Darryl nodded. "Which is why I called you instead."

"If you want me to do something, I'll have the note checked for prints—there won't be any, just yours, I'll bet my life the guy wore gloves—no one else but you has touched it, right?"

"I'm the only one."

"Then fold it up and put it in something, a plastic bag or a clean handkerchief, and I'll take care of things."

"You know someone who'll do this? Without anyone finding out, anyone official?"

"Believe me. I'll get back to you by suppertime."

He took the folded letter out to his car; Darryl had put it into a kerchief, the kerchief into Saran Wrap, the total into a brown paper bag; much better safe than sorry.

At first Escalante thought of visiting the Frog Prince for his wisdom, except Froggie was really an expert on matters medical. Froggie was not the man for this job. Escalante started his car and headed for Henderson, fifteen miles away, where the Lab Rat stayed alive.

The Lab Rat was old now, closing in on seventy, but he'd been as good a technician as any police force in Nevada had, except he was a compulsive and had made some bad desperate moves that got him stripped of his ribbons. He managed to steal enough material when he left to make a small lab for himself in his garage, which is where he was when Escalante drove up at a few minutes after three.

It was a simple enough job. It wouldn't be only if there was a second set of prints on the letter, because that set would belong to the author, more likely than not. Except there wouldn't be more than the one, Escalante knew that. He also knew the Lab Rat was busted from the way he said sure he'd do it, but . . . and then looked off. Escalante had done many somethings for the Lab Rat over the years, but compulsives, sad ones, he was a sucker for, especially when they'd once had real talent. He got out twenty, handed it over, knowing the money would never last 'til sundown.

The nigger McDonald's was jammed with kids because Christmas vacation was already several days old. Escalante sipped his coffee, hoping Millicent wouldn't show, but at four-fifteen she did, shoving in next to him with a Big Mac and fries.

"Too bad you got all that spick blood," Millicent said. "If you was black, I'd bed you good and fast."

"You could make believe."

"Naw—don't think this is racial or nothin', but I never feel folks of the Spanish persuasion are clean. Believe me, you're talking to a housekeeper—I can tell when a spick has been in a room just-like-that."

"Why would I think that was racial or anything?"

"Glad you don't—I gotta eat and run—the Stallone guy is named Danny DeMarco. Suite 3506. He is from a fine old wop family which happens to run vice in Lexington, which is close to Cincinnati and has a lot of vice to run. DeMarco will take over when his old man decides. He is here on a vacation with these two big mothers. He don't go noplace without them; his daddy loves him and he's the son an' heir and nothin' gonna happen to him." She concentrated on her Big Mac, made it disappear.

"How big are they, did you see them?"

"A lot bigger'n you." Now her attention was on the fries. In a blink they had joined the burger.

Millicent slowly began to rise. "That's gotta tide me 'til suppertime," she said. "Don't call me no more for a while."

Escalante put his right hand high.

"And don't fuck with these guys."

He raised his hand higher.

Millicent walked slowly out of the place. Escalante watched. Two ninety-five easy after the snack, and half the men in the place watched her leave. Lustfully.

He stood, went to the pay phone. It was noisier now than ever but that would help, ensure the call was short. He dialed Holly and, when she answered, said, "I lied to you before."

"I know. I told you. I always can tell when you lie."

"I had a contact at The Croesus. Fat black lady in housekeeping. I called her as soon as I'd left you. She owes me so I told her what I needed. She said she'd come up with whatever she could."

"Go on."

"She struck out, Holly. She couldn't find anything."

"Aw, Mex." With such terrible sadness.

"I'm sorry, Holly. Just know I tried."

"Aw, Mex, I hate it when you lie to me."

"I'm in a public phone, there's two guys waiting. I did my best."

"No. You didn't. You lied to me when it counted the most, the most in all my life, Mex; because when he was done with me, when Stallone was finished, he took out a gun and he put it inside me and I don't mean in my mouth, Nikki, and he said 'Listen to me, you got one shot at breathing and that's this: You tell me you love me and if I believe you, I'll let you go.' And I *hated* him so much, and this cold thing was in me and I was bleeding and it hurt but I said 'Oh, God, I love you, I love you so much, I do, I swear, I love you I love you I love you' and he said 'Never shit a shitter' *and he pulled the trigger* and I screamed because I knew my insides were gonna be splattered all over the wallpaper and then I heard the 'click'—his gun wasn't loaded, he was just playing games, some games, right, Nikki? Some fucking games to play with another human—and you sit there knowing who he is and you're gonna let him get away with that—*I wanna sue him* so he can't do it again and you lie and walk away."

He could feel himself weakening until she began to lie herself with the lawsuit business, but he knew he had better get off fast—she was in the top of the class when it came to manipulating. Or at least at manipulating him.

"Tell me his name, Nikki."

"I swear I don't know any more than I told you."

"Okay, liar—just remember this—remember that all the times I told you I cared for you—"

"—I know, I know, you were lying—"

"Wrong—it was true! Every good thing I ever said. And when you were on the bottom, didn't I always climb down there with you? *Didn't I?*"

Then she hung up.

He held the phone, thinking that it was true, she had climbed down, found whatever level he had slipped to. Not many had been brave enough, or stupid enough, to do that. But the truth now, if he had told her, would not have set him free, it more than likely would have killed him, and he wasn't all that sure he was ready for dying yet. Not just yet. Not today. Probably, almost certainly, not today.

It was half past five when he pulled up in the Paxton driveway for the second time that afternoon, took out the brown paper bag with the note inside, rang the bell. Darryl, when he answered, looked no less perturbed, just more surprised. "I was out back with Ashley. By the pool."

"Yours were the only prints," Escalante said; he held out the bag.

Darryl backed away from it. "I don't want that. I don't ever want that in this house again. You can dispose of it, can't you?"

"It won't even be hard."

Darryl looked at him. "You could have saved yourself the trip out here by simply phoning. Why are you here, Nicholas?"

Before he could answer he heard Ashley's voice calling, asking who was there. Darryl excused himself, went out toward the pool, returned a few minutes later. "She wants to see you before you go. I told her you'd stopped by to ask about a child in trouble, and was there room at The Knot."

"That's a better story than I would have come up with."

"I still don't understand why you're here."

"I thought you might feel like talking."

"About . . . ?"

"I got to thinking when I was driving out to have the note checked. You got a lot of threats when your book was published. All kinds of crazies said they'd get you. And I remember on the day we met, you told me you weren't afraid and that I'd know if you ever were afraid, you'd say 'The Reverend says please.' And today you said it. Because of this insanity." He held up the bag, then folded it, shoved it into his back pocket. "I kind of wondered why, after all you've been through, this should knock you sideways, and would you feel better if you talked."

"I'm not sure."

"Up to you. We could mosey into the living room while you make up your mind."

Darryl almost smiled as they walked into the house and the living room off to the right. The room was large, comfortable but spare, with only religious paintings on the walls, Christs, Madonnas, children. "It was the vileness of the writing,'' Darryl said then, going to the gas fireplace, lighting it low. ''No. It was not that. It was just the thing itself. And memory.''

Escalante sat in a chair, watched as Darryl began to pace, a stocky, not all that steady figure, up and down the room. ''Ashley and I were childhood sweethearts. Our parents were success friends and they assumed it would wear off but it didn't. We went to the same high school outside San Francisco, we went to Stanford together, we did religious work together in the summertimes. I've never loved anyone but Ashley, and junior year, thirty years ago, we decided why wait for graduation and divinity school, let's get married now. And during all this time, one of the pleasures we most expected was going to be our children. Ashley was built for birthing, she wanted them more, if anything, than I did. So it did not come as good news . . . it was not a pleasure when I learned that I was then and forever would be sterile. I broke our engagement, I could not inflict my inefficiencies on her. We wept, both of us, and plenty, before deciding to separate the second semester and see how we felt. I did my missionary work in Africa, Ashley did hers in Europe. I was never more miserable and, months later when we met, it turned out she was, too, so we married knowing it would be a barren match. Adoption was never a question—I felt if The Good Lord wanted me sterile, that meant I was not supposed to have babies nearby. Probably a silly and stupid decision, but it didn't seem so at the time. And then today, when that thing arrived, I could not help flashing back through all the bad moments of my life and how they would never have happened if I'd had children of my own. All the drive I had for success, all the fame I insisted on with the television ministry, that was a substitute. I sinned and was punished. And Ashley's afflictions these last years, they are a punishment for *my* sins. I've caused her all her pain. I truly believe that we would have had a wondrous life together if I'd been born like other men, whole, strong, able." He smiled. "I guess it turns out I did want to talk about it. You were good for listening."

Escalante stood. "I would never deprive a fellow American of the right to torment himself, Darryl, but I somehow can't believe there's a direct correlation between happiness and sperm count."

Darryl gave a shrug. "Well, probably one of us is right."

Escalante nodded, walked out to the pool. Ashley was sitting by a round white table, a heavy coat thrown over her shoulders to protect against the chill. She had gotten heavier since the eyelid affliction had begun, but her face was still lovely, the eyes as inviting as ever. And as he approached they were open. "Madam."

"Are you done with Darryl?"

"Our business is completed."

She turned then, took his hands. "What did you think? Oh, Nicholas, he's been upset all day and I know why."

Escalante hesitated, said nothing.

"It's me, it's bearing up under me and the problems I cause him. This morning I was helpless for what seemed like hours and I just fill him with despair—*damn.*"

Escalante watched as suddenly, startlingly, the eyelids locked shut tight. He knew from experience the best thing to do was ignore the spasm, so he said, "I don't think he's upset and if he was, I don't think you have a whole lot to do with it."

She brought her hands up, covered her eyes. "I must have sinned so terribly to bring this on. I've been sitting here wondering just what it was I did and if only there were some way it could be undone." The spasm left. Her eyes were open again. Blinking. "Darryl's being punished for my sins."

"You two should get married," Nick Escalante said.

He was getting the dust off his wooden Magnum when Pinky came calling after eight.

"Sydney to Tahiti," Pinky said as he knocked on the door.

Escalante opened it, answered, "Seven hours, five minutes."

"Damn," Pinky said, walking in, "thought I'd have you sure." He looked at the wooden gun. "So you are going armed."

"Got to accommodate my clients. Lot of competition in my line of work."

"This was it, right? The big five-oh-oh-oh."

Escalante nodded.

"How's it gone?"

"Busier than some."

"I'm glad for that."

Escalante nodded.

Pinky handed over a sloppily wrapped umbrella-shaped package. "In honor of surviving five thousand days," he said. "From Froggie and me."

Escalante, surprised, took the present. He had known Pinchus Zion for ten years and early on decided Pinky had the quickest mind he'd met. Not the brightest—Pinky was a compulsive and no compulsive qualified for brightness.

He'd been head of his class at University of Chicago Law, and his best friend, the Frog Prince, had done equally well at med school. They'd begun coming to Vegas when they were still in college with a roulette system that was fool-proof.

Their first time out they hit for five thousand each. Their second time, they doubled their winnings. By the time they finished their respective grad schools, they were addicted and moved, instead of into major practices in their respective fields, to Vegas.

They made an odd-looking couple, Pinky being short and red-haired, freckled, chubby, while the Frog Prince was dark, muscular, tall, and better looking than anyone since Tyrone Power. Froggie chip-hustled mostly, but when things got bad he'd head for Reno where he made good money jobbing in running one of the biggest emergency wards in the city, often for weeks at a time.

Pinky survived with a different scam: He sued people for peace.

In show business. Pinky knew every deal involving a book, play, movie, song, and anything where plagiarism might be involved. In his office next to Escalante's, he had over three dozen different legal stationeries, all listing him as a senior partner. When news of a sale reached him, he would write the author, explaining with deep regret that a client of his recalled giving the author a similar piece of material for perusal. What happened then was the writer—be it of a song, play, book or film—would inevitably take Pinky's note to *his* lawyer. Proclaiming innocence. This news the writer's lawyer would write to Pinky, who would reply in his next missive that he was sure the writer was pure as any snow yet driven onto the earth, but nonetheless, his client felt wronged and, in spite of his better judgment, Pinky had to follow his client's wishes and would therefore sue.

And then he would wait for the phone call.

It didn't always come but it came enough for his survival. The writer's lawyer would ring up and Pinky would be pleasant and sad because he, Pinky, disliked going to court where reputations might get ruined but he had to follow his client's demands and his client demanded retribution for being plagiarized.

"How much retribution?" the other lawyer would ask.

And then Pinky would hesitate, just before the kill: "I don't think I could get him to settle this thing for less than seventy-five hundred dollars."

"Let me get back to you, I don't think there's a chance of our working this out," the other lawyer would say, and he would meet with his client and say, "I suggest we settle."

"I'm not a plagiarist," the nonplagiarist would say.

"I know," the lawyer would say, "and I also know that if we go into this thing and depositions are taken and all the rest of the legal crap, you're talking thirty thousand dollars *minimum*. Maybe fifty. Now here's a chance to get out of it for seventy-five hundred."

"How?"

"We'll get him to write a letter swearing he never heard of what you wrote and wishing you joy. In exchange, we'll hit him with a check, which is tax-deductible, for probably six thousand, which I'm sure they'll come down to. But *you* decide—just remember, judges are nuts, they don't like artists, you could lose—fifty thousand and stomach-turning anguish against a tax-deductible six, tell me what you want."

"Isn't this what lawyers call blackmail?"

"No; it's what we call settling for peace."

Pinky's scam didn't always work at all. But he sued hundreds of people a year and cleared, on the average, sixty thousand.

As soon as he received a check, he and the Frog Prince would polish up their roulette system. Then head for the tables. They were unusual for compulsives in that they gambled together, shared their funds. They were straight, but they shared an apartment, too, near the Strip. They were together all the time, had been since they were children.

Brilliant, brilliant men except the system never held. Once they had gotten fifty grand ahead. Once in ten years.

"I've decided in honor of your five thousand, fuck it, I'm going after Michael Jackson. A client of mine visited me today and swears he sent 'Billie Jean' to Jackson five years ago."

"Go get 'em, Pinky."

"He's gonna make a hundred mill this year, what's six thousand tax-deductible?" He gestured toward the package. "Open it."

Escalante did, took out a Masai throwing stick, stared at it. Once, years ago, he'd been drunk and started talking on about how someday he was going to have one of his own. They were weapons used by the greatest of African fighting tribes. The sticks weighed several pounds, were close to two feet long, carved from the hardest ebony. One end was sharp and pointed, the other made into a ball-like shape, the size of a small fist. When a Masai had mastered his weapon, he could control the throw and either stun his victim or pierce him through.

"It's a real one," Pinky said.

"I figured."

"Froggie met a sweet lady this summer lived in Nairobi. He got her to find a good one and send it to him."

Escalante ran his hands over the black wood. "Thank you both. Probably you know I'm grateful."

Pinky headed for the door. "Gotta go write Michael Jackson while I'm feeling feisty. I'm glad you lived through today. And don't worry any about the future—another five thousand days here and I promise you'll be dead."

"If I'm lucky."

Pinky waved, zipped out the door. He had all the energy in the world.

Escalante closed the door, sat on his bed, brought the dark wood to his cheek for a moment, then placed it quickly on his bed table. Not the right mood for it now. And he didn't have all that much time. Besides, it was impossible for him to concentrate on the gift—in his mind he heard only Pinky's closing words.

And he could not stop thinking of Holly.

There were many unusual things about Cyrus Kinnick but nothing as extraordinary as this: He had a shorter, more scraggly and even less flattering beard than Yassir Arafat and Escalante never conceived that such a thing was possible.

Kinnick stood under six feet and could not have weighed over 125 pounds. Even the clearly expensive Ivy League–styled grey suit couldn't disguise the almost emaciated body beneath. Dark hair cut short, dark bright blue eyes, he moved stiffly and when they shook hands at nine o'clock at the Grand, Escalante was aware of the softness of Kinnick's flesh.

Making a quick assessment, he decided Kinnick had probably been the brightest kid in school and always, always, the last one chosen in the playground. And more than likely, the playground was where he had wanted to excel. Late twenties, rich and weird—inside of five minutes Escalante had glimpsed the pistol in Kinnick's shoulder holster.

And inside of five minutes more he realized that he had never met a man as timid or afraid or panicked, somewhere in there, as Cyrus Kinnick. His eyes flicked constantly, the least sudden sound—a slot machine bell—brought a reaction. "I hadn't realized the Grand was so big, I never would have booked here if I'd known; I don't much want to gamble here."

"The noise bothers people sometimes."

"I don't mind noise," Kinnick said quickly.

Escalante nodded.

"Have you any suggestions?"

"Silver Spoon is smaller. Just down the block."

"All right, then."

They left the Grand, walked right to the sidewalk, then left and they were halfway to the Silver Spoon when a car pulled up beside them and a woman said, "Wanna blowjob?"

"No, thank you, Katherine," Escalante said.

She squinted. "I can't see shit without my glasses, that you, Nikki?"

"It is."

"Well, happy holidays." She drove away.

Kinnick stared after her. "Welcome to Las Vegas," he said.

"More churches and eagle scouts per capita than any other city in the country, if you can believe the chamber of commerce, something I wouldn't make a habit of doing."

"Do people actually say yes to her?"

"Apparently she's very ardent. She has a devoted following—usually she just parks, but being that it's a slow week, she has to hustle."

Kinnick shook his head and in a few minutes they were

at the Silver Spoon. Kinnick looked around a moment, nodded approval, moved in his quick, nervous way toward the nearest crap table, watched, shook his head after a few minutes, went to the next.

Escalante followed along, grateful for only one thing: Kinnick wasn't a talker. His mood, not high all day, was dropping rapidly. Five thousand nights now. Tomorrow would be his five-thousand-and-first morning. Pinky was wrong when he said not to worry, he'd never last five thousand more.

Right then, Escalante didn't see himself surviving five hundred more. Or, when you really pushed it, fifty. And he wasn't sure, right then he truly was not sure, if he cared.

Then Kinnick started to gamble and Escalante's mood took a sudden turn and headed straight off the cliff. Kinnick was a "don't" bettor: He bet against the crapshooter. If the shooter began his roll with a seven or eleven he won; the "don't" bettor lost. In other words, a "don't" bettor was siding with the casino.

It was a conservative way to play, as sound as any. Kinnick put down a hundred dollars for his first bet. The dice were hot and it took five minutes before the next shooter had a chance. Kinnick won his bet, saved fifty, and now bet a hundred and fifty.

It was madness. Escalante had had many jobs where he was simply window-dressing. Some asshole wants to impress a girl so he hires a bodyguard for the evening out. But nobody who started out with a hundred-dollar bet needed protecting.

At ten o'clock Kinnick was dead even and wanted a drink. They went to the bar. Fucking Perrier drinker, Escalante decided before they sat. The waitress came, took their orders for Escalante's beer, Kinnick's Perrier.

"You gamble?"

Escalante shrugged.

"I love it."

Escalante shrugged again.
"How'd you get into this line of work?"
"Dull story."
Their drinks came.
"Were you in 'Nam?" Kinnick asked.
Escalante shook his head.
"I figured maybe you learned your work in 'Nam."
"Viet," Escalante said.
"Hmm?"
"Everybody calls it fucking ' 'Nam' like it was a fraternity name. Were you in 'Delt'? I decided to call it Viet. Yes, I was in Viet."
"You're very touchy, aren't you?"
"I'm always like this when I'm protecting a client; there's so much danger lurking, if you get slaphappy, that's when trouble starts."
They went back to the crap tables in a while, and Kinnick upped his bets to two hundred. And Escalante stood there, wondering if he could last 'til eleven. If it had been an ordinary day, no problem, but this wasn't, and this situation was not your ordinary situation, protecting a nervous scarecrow who carried a gun and who sometimes bet as much as two hundred and fifty dollars on a single roll of the dice.
And don't forget the lie about the friend and recommender in Boston.
And don't forget Holly and her lies either. And Escalante realized he had to confront her before the day ended, whatever the consequences might prove to be, and there would be, he knew, deadly consequences, and when they were on their second round, at a little after eleven, Escalante said, "We're quits, all right?"
Kinnick looked at him then. So strangely. "What in the world do you mean?"
"There's a place I've got to go."
"But—I intend gambling for hours."

"I haven't got hours."

Kinnick's nervousness grew—his fingers went to his scraggly beard, tried finding hairs to pull at. "I thought you were hired at my discretion—I haven't made any other arrangements for this evening—"

"Kinnick, listen, nothing has to change—I promise you can gamble right here as long as your money holds out—"

"—but—my safety—"

"—I'll make you another promise: No one will mug you *in* the casino. And outside, they've got these yellow things called taxicabs—you just tell them where you want to go and in thirty seconds they'll have you back at the Grand, all safe and dry—"

"—but I need protecting—I need . . . you—"

"—you only think you do, good-bye, Kinnick," and then he was up and gone from the bar and a few minutes after that he was in his car, gunning through the night toward 1108 Chestnut and then he was pounding on the door, shouting Holly's name until she answered and let him in. "You been calling me a liar all day and you were right, but now I'm going to start calling you a liar, too, that's all right, isn't it? Danny DeMarco is the Stallone figure in your life and he's at The Croesus, room 3506."

"You never yet failed me."

"I've failed you plenty. Good night, Holly." He started for the door.

"Wait."

"Why?"

"Jesus, don't get so huffy, at least let me write it down."

"Write it down."

She got a pad and pencil. "You know how he spells it?"

"No."

"Thirty-five-oh-six, did you say?"

"That's what I said, good night, Holly."

"You just got here, Mex."

"Good luck on your goddam lawsuit."

"What are you acting so angry for?"
"Liar."
"I'm not."
"You never once intended suing the son of a bitch, did you, sweetness?"
"I'm gonna do it."
"Sure you are."
"You'll see—a man does a thing like he did, a human being gets humiliated, sullied, he can't go around loose—"
"—I won't help you anymore. I don't help liars—"
"—quit calling me that, Mex—"
"—quit *doing* it, then—" and now he put his big hands on her shoulders and began to squeeze. "Tell the truth."
"I am—"
"—liar—but I can make you stop—if I said I'd help you if you stopped lying, you'd stop lying—"
"—would you?—help?—"
"—tell the truth for once and we'll see—"
"—I need for you to help me—"
"—what kind of help?—want me to hustle you up a good lawyer for your legendary lawsuit?—"
"—no—"
"—what, then?—what kind of help could I give you?—"
"—you know—"
"—tell me—"
"—I need you—"
"—for *what?*—"
"—for what you can do—"
"—the lawsuit was bullshit, admit that—"
"—I'll admit anything you want if you say you'll help me—why do you think I called you—nobody else can do what you can do—"
"—and get killed—"
"—there's only three of them—"
"—three of them with guns—"
"—you gotta do it—you gotta go in there and beat the shit out of them and give me my chance—"

"—for what?—"

"—I want his nuts in my hands!—"

"—and the lawsuit?—"

"—was bullshit—"

"—and if they kill me?—"

"—I'll be miserable for days—"

"—that's the gold-star girl I knew—"

"—I want DeMarco so bad for what he did—I need revenge, Mex—"

"—I'm good at revenge—"

"—you'll help me, then?—you'll help me get his nuts in my hands?—"

"I've always been a sucker for religious crusades," Nick Escalante said. . . .

# PART II

# The Mex in Motion

# CHAPTER 1
# The Envy of All Mankind

When the bell rang to suite 3506, Kinlaw looked first at his watch—it was just after two in the morning—and then at Tiel. "What the fuck you think?" Kinlaw asked.

"I think it's the bell, asshole," Tiel answered.

"I know it's the bell, 'course it's the bell, I got ears, I know what a bell sounds like, I meant, what the fuck you think *it is,* you 'specting anything?"

Tiel shook his head, gestured toward the bedroom door.

Kinlaw looked at the door, not quite closed. DeMarco never closed the door all the way when he was banging. You could hear things. DeMarco was in there with some dark meat and Kinlaw hoped he wouldn't be offered seconds. You could never tell what they had but you knew they had something. "What about the bedroom door?"

"Not the door—what's *behind* the door—Danny—maybe *he*'s expecting someone."

The bell rang again, longer this time.

"Hey, shit-for-brains," Tiel said then, "don't let it ring anymore."

"You mean answer?"

"Hey, you're smartening up every day, it's wonderful."

Kinlaw got up from the TV area, moved slowly to the door, instinctively touching the pistol inside his jacket as he went. Someday he was going to have it out with Tiel. Just the two of them alone in some room. Everybody thought they were buddies 'cause they looked alike, same size, age, blond. But Tiel thought Kinlaw was dumb and he was gonna pay for that sooner or later.

Kinlaw opened the door, looked out. He saw a weird-looking greaseball. Naw, he wasn't weird-*looking,* it was his getup. Lizard boots and black leather pants and a black leather jacket open down to the belt, and lotsa rings and there was a piece of gold jewelry that must have weighed a ton hanging from a gold chain around his neck. Biggest goddam piece of jewelry, almost round, only not quite.

"You want somethin'?"

"To see Mr. DeMarco," the greaseball said.

"Abow?"

"Personal."

"Gotta 'pointment?"

"No."

"'S bizzy."

"I'll wait."

"Not inside, you're not." Kinlaw started to close the door.

"I don't think Baby would be too happy with me stuck out here."

I know that name from somewhere, Kinlaw thought, as he slammed the door right in the greaseball's face.

Tiel was watching the tube when Kinlaw came back. From behind the bedroom door now there were cries of the nigger with DeMarco. That meant he was almost done banging her. He liked to come at the same time as the hookers. Tiel tried to concentrate on the movie—a Mario Lanza musical for Chrissakes, but then it was late and there wasn't much choice. He hoped DeMarco didn't offer seconds on the nigger. It wasn't so much that Tiel didn't like seconds or that he didn't like sharing the seconds with Kinlaw; the truth was, what he enjoyed more than the sex was like with the girl the night before, punishing her on the service stairs afterward. Watching girls fold, that was the best. He looked up now. "Well?"

"I took care of it," Kinlaw said. "Easy."

"I don't like the sound of that; there's nothing you can take care of 'easy.' Who was at the door?"

"Greaseball. Wanted DeMarco but didn't have nothing set up so I let him cool it outside. Friend of Baby's."

Tiel stood up fast. "He said he was a friend of Baby and you let him wait outside?"

Kinlaw nodded. "He didn't have no 'pointment. An' he wouldn't say about what."

Tiel started for the door. "Baby doesn't just run this hotel, y'know—the *town,* Kinlaw. If anybody does, Baby does, and it's not smart getting his buddies pissed, okay?" He adjusted his jacket, hurried to the door, looked out at the guy in the black leather. Maybe a greaseball, could be a wop. The jewelry was more wop. Great big gold thing hanging from the chain. At first he thought it was like one of those kike stars but this one had more sides, eight probably. "You friends with Baby?"

"I didn't say friends. But we go back fifteen years."

"And you're . . . ?"

"Nick."

"Now what's this all about? I'll let you wait inside, you tell me. Maybe I will."

"Girl."

"You got a girl for Mr. DeMarco?"

"I want to talk to him about a girl."

"Pretty? He likes 'em pretty and he likes 'em slim; if they're not, forget it."

"You just described her."

Tiel stared down at the dark-skinned guy. Tiel stood six five and weighed 250 but there was something he didn't like about the guy's looks. No. More an attitude. He didn't move when he talked. Still. All the time still. But what the hell—the guy obviously wasn't carrying anything and both he and Kinlaw had heat. DeMarco too. It was dumb to worry about a wop with flashy jewelry, so he gestured for the guy to wait inside.

As he closed the door Tiel could hear Danny and the nigger crying out as they came.

DeMarco lay naked on the bed, watching as the girl dressed. His old man would have gone off like a rocket if he'd known; his old man wanted nothing to do with the colored and Danny had never had one 'til tonight. She had managed to stay with him pretty good. And she didn't smell at all, except for her perfume, which was nice.

"Jesse, that your name?"

She nodded.

He looked at her. She was pretty, like the club singer, whatever the hell her name was, Carroll something. No. Diahann Carroll. And he was a ringer for Stallone. He should really knock her up, their children would be something to see. "Ready for another round?"

She smiled, held out her hands. "I'm still shaking from what you just did to me."

"I can go all night. I never get tired."

She nodded again. "I believe that."

"I'll be coming to town a lot now—twice a year, more maybe."

"I'm usually at the Silver Spoon."

"You know who I am?"

"I just know you're the king of the sack."

"I run Lexington, Kentucky."

She looked at him. "Wow. You must be older than you look."

"Twenty-four. My old man helps me." But his old man was sick. What he'd told her wasn't true. But he *would* be in charge before he was twenty-seven. Unless the goddam doctors were lying. And then he wouldn't be stuck with shit like Tiel and Kinlaw. Fucking animals. But his old man wouldn't stop worrying over him. His old man had too many enemies and one way to get at him would be through the son. Ridiculous. He could take care of anything that came for him. If it was a man. If it was a woman, give him half an hour and they were begging for more.

Jesse finished her quick dressing, stood. "This was some night," she said.

DeMarco grabbed her hand, held it tight, started to twist, wondered if he should have a little fun. Probably dumb. At least with this chocolate drop. They didn't have the stuff to make it interesting, they folded up too easy. He dropped her hand, let her go. She smiled at him, left the room. He lay there naked, his fingers fondling The Envy of All Mankind.

When he began to twist her hand, Jesse thought she was in trouble. He was the kind who liked to hurt women, she could tell that from the way he roughed her around during the sex. But she got through that with as good a job of bullshitting as she had in her, making him think she thought he was some wild stallion when the reality was close to that of a raging Chihuahua.

While she was dressing her hands *were* trembling because what she wanted to do was run. Now, as she left the bedroom, that urge was on her again. She controlled it, entered the main room of the suite, smiled at the two giant blonds—

—and then she saw Escalante standing in the corner of the room. She almost said hello to him, quickly realized he didn't want the recognition.

What the hell was he doing with this kind of garbage?

Then she had it, and she picked up her pace, because her pill supplier worked nights at the emergency room of Memorial and he had told her about Hollister being brought in the night before. These must be the ones who had worked her over.

Jesse got the doorknob to turn on her second try and

when she was out in the corridor she finally allowed herself to run for the elevator, jam the goddam button. She wanted far away from 3506, before there was blood on the moon.

As soon as the girl was gone, Tiel went to the bedroom door, knocked. "Yeah, come in."

DeMarco was lying naked on the rumpled bed, touching himself.

Pig, Tiel thought.

DeMarco lay there, watching Tiel try not to watch him. Jealous bastard, DeMarco thought. "Yeah, what?"

"Guy outside wants to see you."

"Who?"

"Don't know—but he knows Baby a long time, and he wants to see you about some girl."

DeMarco sat, rubbed his chest. Baby might be sending him a present. Possible. Probably not but if it was, she'd be worth it. "I'll be out in a while," DeMarco said.

Tiel nodded, left.

DeMarco went to the bathroom and splashed on some Brut. If it was good enough for Namath, how could you argue? He grabbed his silk robe, put it over his naked muscular body, tied it loosely at the waist, walked barefoot into the living room of the suite.

As soon as he entered he knew it wasn't some present from Baby. Baby wouldn't be seen with scum like the fink in the lizard boots and the black leather joke costume and the jewelry. He put on a big smile, held out his hand. "Any friend of Baby's . . ."

"It's good of you to see me like this, Mr. DeMarco."

"You can call me Danny, what do I call you?"

"Nick."

After they shook, DeMarco kept the smile on, walked to the desk, stood behind it. "Well, Nick, I'm told there's something about a girl."

"Yessir."

"I'm a big fan of the female sex, and that includes girls." He laughed a little. "But only if they're of the pretty variety, yours pretty?"

"Was."

"Again?" He looked at the greaseball hard now, saw the effect of his stare as the guy began to let his nervousness show.

"Last night, Mr. DeMarco—a dear friend of mine was shown some disrespect, and I thought that, you know, maybe something might be done about it."

"Disrespect? Sorry, Nick, but like I said, I'm a fan of girls, you got the wrong room. I'm a strict gentleman when it comes to the ladies."

"I don't think it was so gentlemanly, what you did."

"And what did I do, Nick?" DeMarco sat down at the desk, enjoying himself now, looking at the chili picker stand there with Tiel and Kinlaw behind him.

"She says you took a weapon, a pistol, and inserted it into her private parts and frightened her bad."

"That's not disrespect, Nick, that's a game, we were having a party."

"Well, from her point of view, it was not very enjoyable. And what happened after, she also didn't like much."

"You better tell me about that in detail, Nick; was it another game?" He waited as the jerk in leather glanced around at Tiel and Kinlaw.

"No point to detail, I don't know much detail, she doesn't remember all that much, except she had to be treated and stitched up in the emergency ward of Memorial."

DeMarco looked at the blonds. "Any of this ring a bell with you? Tiel? Kinlaw?"

"No, Mr. DeMarco," Tiel said, Kinlaw echoing.

"They're lying, Nick."

"I know. This is probably another game you're playing, only this time it's with me."

"Very good, Nick. Let me remember back a minute—you

said that there was disrespect shown and you thought something might be done about it, I got that right?''

''You do, yessir.''

''In the first place, you can't show disrespect to a whore, and that's what your friend is, right, Nick?''

''She's a very ladylike human being.''

''And you're her pimp, right, Nick?''

''Oh, no, Mr. DeMarco.''

''What are you, then?—coming in here with that asshole costume—you look like a two-bit spick pimp to me.''

''You got me all wrong.''

''What do you do, Nick, if you're not a pimp.''

''Various things; I like to think I'm in the people business.''

''The 'people business'?'' DeMarco had to laugh. ''I never heard it called that before.'' He looked at the guy in leather. ''Are you from fucking Mars?''

''No, sir, I'm just here because a dear friend of mine—''

''—shut up, Nick, okay?''

''Yessir.''

DeMarco got up from behind the desk. ''Here's my reading, Nick—a pimp has one of his girls get bruised, she can't work, he's dumb enough to ask for money to cover his losses.''

''You got me all wrong, Mr. DeMarco, I'm legit,'' and he reached into the right hand pocket of the leather jacket, brought out some celluloid. ''Look—see?—credit cards, American Express, Diners, they're mine.''

''You *are* from Mars.'' He looked at Tiel and Kinlaw. ''What do you think?''

''Whatever you do,'' Tiel said, Kinlaw echoing.

''What the hell, maybe he's got a point.'' DeMarco opened the desk drawer, brought out a packet of money in a rubber band. ''This is twenty thousand, would that cover the disrespect?''

''You're very generous.''

''And you're very stupid.'' He dropped the money back

into the drawer, brought out a pistol. "But even though you're stupid, probably you know what this is."

The greaseball nodded.

"See, it's got a silencer and everything—I could blow your kneecaps away and they wouldn't even know it in the next room."

The spick could not take his eyes off the weapon.

DeMarco put the gun back alongside the money, closed the drawer. "There's gonna be no cash changing hands here, Nick, but don't be disappointed, because something very important is going to be talked about—your future."

"Let me just leave, how's that?"

"Oh, I'm going to, the question is: In what condition will you leave and how much pain are you going to be in tomorrow? Now you have a choice, Nick, old friend: I can say bye and wave and you walk out free as air, or I can have my amigos here break you up bad, which do you want?"

"Free as air."

"I figured that. But if I do that, if I'm generous, if I'm so sweet to you, I'd want people to know about it and you'd have to tell them. Let me hear you, Nick—say right now how sweet I am. And if I like it, you're free as air."

"You're a very fine man, Mr. DeMarco. A peach. You're generous, you don't hold grudges, you're the best, a real top-of-the-line human being."

"Not good enough, try again," DeMarco said. "Talk about my good qualities. This is it for you, Nick. Your last shot. I'm waiting."

Nothing from the greaseball.

DeMarco studied the spick in leather, wondering what the hell was going on behind his eyes.

Still silence.

*"What are you thinking about?"*

". . . Scotland . . ."

DeMarco blinked.

". . . Scotland but it went away. . . ."

"He's crazy," DeMarco said, and he gave the sign to Tiel and Kinlaw. "Let him go—don't hurt him—just see our friend Nick to the elevator."

"This way, Nick," Tiel said, moving toward the pimp. Out of habit he tapped his piece inside his jacket, wondering if the guy would be trouble or not. Not. Too scared. He'd probably try and talk them out of it once they were on the service stairs.

Kinlaw looked at the asshole in leather and all he hoped was that it would go easy, that the jerk would be stupid enough to get between him and Tiel. It wouldn't happen, no one was that dumb, to get caught in the middle, but it would be nice, less work.

They started toward the door then, and Kinlaw stared as the guy let Tiel take the lead, fell in behind him, let Kinlaw move in last. The guy had his back to Kinlaw. Moving slow, back turned, right smack in the middle. Kinlaw almost smiled, took a breath, relaxed a little, started the move for his gun.

It was enough to make you believe in God.

# CHAPTER 2

# Eighteen Seconds

"You're a very fine man, Mr. DeMarco. A peach." Nick Escalante hurried on. "You're generous, you don't hold grudges, you're the best, a real top-of-the-line human being."

"Not good enough, try again. Talk about my good qualities. This is it for you, Nick. Your last shot. I'm waiting."

Escalante stood there in his pimp clothes staring at the Stallone-like figure. So far the evening had gone along pretty much as he had thought it might. The pimp story had done its job, because he wanted to talk to them first, not just barge in swinging. It always helped—at least it always helped *him*—to dislike the enemy. You didn't need to have a hate on. But contempt was good. Disgust was better. And loathing perhaps best of all.

And he felt that trinity for the men in the room, for their words toward him, their actions toward Holly. All of that had worked out fine.

He just didn't want to fight them.

There was no fear involved. Of course the blonds were extraordinarily powerful. And young. And professional. And they enjoyed their work, if Holly was any example. And they would do a better job on him, no question. Break him apart, slowly, really do a workup on him. But he had suffered pain and often in the past, he had been blown apart in the past and *that* was pain nothing these two could approach.

No, he felt no fear for Tiel or Kinlaw. He felt... just so tired of it all. The lashing out, the violence. Five thousand days can make a man weary of anything. Maybe if he took the beating, got busted up for one month or six, he'd have time to think, reorder whatever had once been his priorities.

It suddenly didn't matter to him whether he was still the master of edged weapons. Escalante stood motionless, thinking that over and over, because once, of course, it had mattered, as much as anything. Now he wondered why.

So let them work him over. He would do his best to nullify the pain. Where would he go? Scotland! Yes, Scotland, he had had several customers from Scotland over the years and he pumped them when he could, and he knew, if you were hitchhiking with nothing but a knapsack and a world of time, that the most beautiful way to enter Scotland was via the A 68 because you're over a thousand feet up then, when you come to the town of Carter Bar, and the Lowlands, if the weather is clear, well, the Lowlands spread out for you to infinity.

And Edinburgh. With Princes Street, the most beautiful, everybody thought so, the without doubt most beautiful main street of any city in the world, what with the shops lining one side while just across was a great hill with the Castle on top, and when you visited the Castle and looked out, the view made even the sight of the Lowlands ordinary.

And the A 96. You walked it as it curved toward Inverness and eventually you found yourself looking at a lake, none other than Loch Ness, where Nessie had been outwitting the world for centuries.

And on you walked, north, always north because you had to see the Highlands, nothing on earth had an edge on the Highlands, the way the great mounds curved down to the road, tricking you, making you think they were thousands of feet higher than they were.

And the Isle of Skye, where the people were so kind to visitors, because there were so few and they only came for one reason, the tranquillity, and in an afternoon you could make more friends on Skye than in five thousand days spent other places.

And then finally head back down, and the one great

splurge would be near the town of Fort William because that was where Inverlochy Castle stood. A real castle with perhaps a dozen rooms for guests, and a kitchen that ranked with any in Britain, and everything was cooked perfectly but if you could improve on perfection, and they tried at Inverlochy Castle, it was their grouse, with the skin a crackling brown and you ordered only the finest wine to go with it, probably a Burgundy—

—a red Burgundy—

—Burgundy the color of blood—

—and now as he stared at DeMarco, Escalante felt himself starting to lose control. The castle began to recede. And he knew what was happening to him.

His reptile brain was taking over.

Most people don't know it, no reason they should, but every human on this earth has, inside his skull, a reptile brain. There was a doctor or a scientist, McLean or something like that, that Escalante had read about one time, and it had always stuck with him. The reptile brain is a remnant from an earlier millennium, and over time, what we think of as our brain has grown, on top of and surrounding the older cells of the reptile brain.

Our reptile brain is always with us. No surgery can ever take it away. And it has but five urges: It wants to sleep. And eat. And fight and fuck and kill. There are no cells for caring in the reptile brain. No cells for friendship, love. Those are all in the surrounding brain, the one we use.

Most of the time, but not all. Because buried in the moist darkness is the reptile brain. It has always been there, as it will always be. In all of us. Waiting. . . .

*"What are you thinking about?"*

". . . Scotland . . . Scotland but it went away. . . ."

"He's crazy," DeMarco said.

The Mex saw him make the sign to Tiel and Kinlaw.

"Let him go—don't hurt him—just see our friend Nick to the elevator."

Escalante saw Tiel move toward him, instinctively touching inside his jacket where his pistol was waiting. He glanced at Kinlaw, too, then moved between the two men, because one of the principles of the chapter called "Give In to Win" in the MacShane book *Our Friend Violence* was that if you were going into battle with skilled opposition the best thing to do was often the worst thing to do—everyone knew the worst place to be was between your enemies, so if you went there, intentionally put yourself in jeopardy, there would be a gift given back to you, a respite in the enemies' concentration, a moment of overconfidence.

Escalante could feel now what he always felt just before combat: heat, heat emanating from his groin area.

"This way, Nick," Tiel said.

Escalante let Tiel lead the way toward the door. He followed, giving Kinlaw, a step behind, a clear shot at him. They moved slowly. They had him just where he wanted them.

The heat in his groin increased, because if you knew violence, if you understood it and were as skilled as they all were, you knew it wasn't like a Bruce Lee movie where lethal blows had the effect of drops of rain. Expert violence went fast because the body was infantlike in its vulnerability. If you were comfortable with the knowledge of where to attack, then all of what was about to happen, win or lose, shouldn't take long: When he was in his prime it would end in half a minute, less on a good day.

Now his reptile brain had him totally. The heat was intense. Violence was closing in but violence could be your friend, and Escalante couldn't help it, some men drove fast cars brilliantly, some were good at money, he seemed most alive when pain was in the air.

> It began, the first second of it, with nothing unusual about it. In fact, no one knew, except Escalante, that it had begun at all. DeMarco, seated at the desk perhaps fifteen feet across

the room, was watching with interest, his head cocked to the left. Kinlaw was reaching for his gun as he moved close in behind the greaseball's back. Tiel in the front was also reaching for his piece when he heard an unexpected sound—a grunt, surely from Kinlaw, a few feet behind him. The reason for the sound was this: Escalante had snap-kicked backward with his right lizard boot, aiming and hitting Kinlaw's left kneecap. The boot was heavy but it also had a sharp metal heel covering. Escalante knew two things from the sound of the heel hitting: that Kinlaw would scream, but not 'til the third second, and that Kinlaw's kneecap was gone.

During second number two, DeMarco sat at the desk, hearing the grunt, not quite understanding the why of its existence. His head was still cocked to one side. If he did anything it was simply that he blinked several times in quick succession. Kinlaw, for his part, felt nothing much: His entire giant's body was, for that instant, numb. Tiel, in the lead, quickened the movement with his right hand for his weapon while at the same time commencing to turn his enormous body in order to catch sight of whatever was going on. Escalante did little, took a quick step forward, away from Kinlaw, toward Tiel.

Not a great deal happened during the third second. Escalante continued his move, only now he took his right hand, brought it in front of his body and then to the right of it. DeMarco widened his eyes into a stare. Tiel, his gun half out, was almost finished with his turn. And the knowledge of what had happened to his kneecap reached Kinlaw's brain and he began to scream and scream.

The fourth second was terribly important. It was the first time DeMarco realized the need for movement and he began to stand. Kinlaw, deep in pain, began to fold. Escalante, his right hand out and to the right of his body, moved it toward Tiel's face. The hand held his credit cards and they were real, or had been, they were outdated now, and the edges had been whittled to a certain degree of sharpness so that as he slashed the cards with great quickness and power across Tiel's forehead, they caused a quick curtain of blood to descend and Tiel was, at least for the moment, blind.

The fifth second was crucial to Nick Escalante. He moved faster than he yet had, back toward Kinlaw, grabbing him, holding him upright, moving next to Kinlaw so that the giant was behind him and he pulled Kinlaw's arms tight around his own body. DeMarco was up now while Tiel tried, with absolute lack of success, to blink the blood away.

In the sixth second, Kinlaw, held upright, screamed again, while Escalante did very little, simply dropped his head to his chest. DeMarco shouted for the first time: "Stop him" was the best he could come up with as Tiel brought his hands up, the gun in one of them, and tried to make the blood stop streaming down into his stinging eyes.

Second seven: Escalante, with all the strength he had, snapped his head back at a slight angle, his skull careening into several parts of Kinlaw's face, most notably the nose and the cheekbone. DeMarco moved to open the desk drawer. Tiel began swearing in blind frustration.

In the eighth second Escalante stepped away from Kinlaw and the blond, his face shattered, began to slide to the floor. DeMarco got his hands on the desk drawer with the gun inside. Tiel continued, incoherently, to swear.

Second nine was uneventful in the extreme. Tiel swiped out blindly with his pistol. Kinlaw made it, semiconscious, to the floor, DeMarco got the desk drawer open as Escalante made two quick steps toward Tiel.

The tenth second was the end for Tiel as Escalante drove a short blow toward the bleeding man's Adam's apple. Although the blow was short, it had a terrifying power and accuracy of delivery and the knuckles, edged, ended Tiel's voice box and did little for his air-gathering capacities. DeMarco at last got his hands on his gun with the silencer.

The eleventh second was when Nick Escalante launched into his dive. His body for a moment was parallel to the rug as he brought his right hand toward his chest. Tiel staggered back, trying to stay conscious. Kinlaw rolled on the floor, one hand to his kneecap, the other covering his face as DeMarco brought the gun up and got ready to fire.

DeMarco fired in the twelfth second, the bullet passing where Escalante had been before he began his dive. Tiel staggered, holding his throat, the gun dropping from his hands. Kinlaw continued to roll on the floor as Escalante ripped, with his right hand, the heavy octagonal piece of gold jewelry from the breakaway clasp that held it to the thin gold chain.

He landed on his left shoulder during the thirteenth second and began a quick roll up to one knee. DeMarco held the pistol as it recoiled in his hands. Tiel joined Kinlaw, both of them doing strange motions as they lay on the floor of the suite in The Croesus Hotel.

DeMarco fired his second shot during the fourteenth second. Again his aim was faulty, being behind his target. Tiel and Kinlaw were much as before. Escalante was now up on one knee, his right hand holding the heavy piece of octagonally shaped gold.

In the fifteenth second Escalante realized that he was, without question, going to win. Certain moves had to be completed, yes, but he was so skilled at them that the chances of a third shot hitting him or even being fired were next to impossible. He was about a dozen feet from DeMarco when he backhanded the gold toward the man who looked like Sylvester Stallone. He could have gone for the eyes or the nose, but because DeMarco was a talker, he decided, symbolically perhaps, that the mouth was the proper target. DeMarco stood still after his second shot, the pistol recoiling in his hands. There was nothing to report new in the movements of Kinlaw or Tiel: They were done.

It took less than a second for the gold octagon to strike, so calling it second sixteen is not strictly accurate but will have to do. Escalante stayed on one knee as the heavy object struck DeMarco's mouth, knocking out the two top front teeth, continuing on, wedging itself over his tongue, tearing both sides of his mouth, blood spurting as his balance was taken from him.

Second seventeen: Escalante got to his feet. DeMarco was out of control, falling helplessly over the back of the chair.

Final and eighteenth second: Escalante stood. DeMarco landed hard, his head slamming against the corner behind the desk where the wall and floor came together, out of it; Tiel and Kinlaw as before.

How did Escalante feel just then? He didn't know. He was perspiring as he turned in a circle, looking down at the three figures on the floor. He could sense his heart. And there was still the heat in his groin, so his reptile brain hadn't gone yet, he was almost certain of that.

He was positive when, without really his knowing, a cry came from his throat, loud and rough, a cry of . . . of what? He was almost embarrassed by the sound. (The reptile brain was retreating now, quickly, going, going, but never totally gone.)

A cry of continuance perhaps. Clearly, from the evidence on the floor around him, whatever it was he was once, he remained.

Besides, what was so terrible about victory?

He got to work then in silence. At least *he* was silent. Around him, from the other three, rasps or sounds of pain. He took a coil of catgut from one pocket, cut it with a sharp ring he hadn't needed to use, took the blonds, bound their feet together, then their hands together, lying on the floor back to back. He tied them so that if they struggled, and he doubted they had much in them but if they did, the bonds would only grow tighter. Next he gathered up their guns along with DeMarco's, put them in a pile on a glass tabletop. He reached for his gold octagon after that, cleaned the blood from it, put it back on the gold chain around his neck. Last he picked DeMarco up, tied him hand and foot to the desk chair. Finally he went to the phone, dialed the booth in the corner of the lobby downstairs where Holly was waiting, told her to come on up when she answered, went to the window and stared out at the December night until she knocked.

He opened 3506 and she stepped inside, the veiled hat covering her battered face. They had parted two hours before, when he agreed to help her, because she had to "get ready," whatever that meant. He went to his place to change and she picked him up in her car, which she said had her luggage in the trunk. They drove to The Croesus and she was worried about going in, did the veil make her stand out? He took her to the phone booth, assured her no one would notice, told her to wait for half an hour and if he hadn't called by then, he never would. She nodded.

Now as she entered the suite she looked around, her stare resting on DeMarco. Holly watched him for a long time. Then she said, "Yeah, that's the guy."

"Jesus, it better be; if it isn't, he's got one hell of a lawsuit."

DeMarco was coming out of his daze now. He blinked slowly. Both sides of his mouth still bled, the blood making paths down to his chin, dripping from there to the robe.

Holly took off her hat with the veil, put it with her purse on top of the TV set. She was wearing dark slacks and a paisley blouse. Her body was fine, trim as ever, except when she moved it was clear she was still badly hurt. She moved now to DeMarco. "Remember me?"

DeMarco hesitated. "Sure. 'Course. You're the party girl we had all that fun with last night."

"Right. And I had so much fun I can't stand the party's being over. I want to keep it going forever, you know what I mean?"

Escalante took a step backward, watched them.

DeMarco blinked, looked at him. "What's she up to?"

Escalante shook his head, watched Holly, said nothing.

Holly knelt beside DeMarco then, opened his robe. "The Envy of All Mankind," she said.

DeMarco was coming to faster now. "You know who I am?"

"Sure I do," Holly said. "You're the party-giver." And now she stood, moved slowly back to the TV, hesitated a moment, opened her purse and reached inside.

Christ! Escalante thought, staring as she lifted a large pair of garden shears out of her purse, snapped them together hard, the metallic click enough to make the blonds stop moaning.

*"What the fuck is she doing?"* DeMarco shouted.

Escalante stood silent, wondering himself.

"Is this about money?—" DeMarco stared at Escalante. "Is that what all this is, sure it is, take it, take the twenty for Chrissakes."

"What twenty?" Holly asked.

"Twenty thousand. Top desk drawer."

Holly went to the drawer, lifted the bundle of cash with the rubber band around it, flipped it across the room to Escalante. "It's not about money," she said then. "It's about love."

And now as she snapped the garden shears together again, moving in on DeMarco, he began to scream out—"It wasn't me—I didn't do nothing—*they* did it—both of them—Kinlaw and Tiel were the ones."

Bad form, Escalante thought. If you were involved with the Combination, that sort of totally chickenshit behavior was not much esteemed.

"After," Kinlaw, the only one who could talk, whispered. "...we didn't have our turn 'til after...."

"You shut up!" Holly said, whirling on the blond giant.

Escalante stared at her. She was embarrassed. After all she'd told him about what had happened to her in this room last night, there was worse she couldn't bring herself to tell. For a moment, his gold-star girl was there in the suite with him—for the first time, he was glad he had done what he'd done.

Holly moved toward DeMarco now, knelt beside him. "I hope I sharpened these enough," she said, "I do hope so, let's see," and very slowly, with surgical care, she took hold of DeMarco's limp penis, pulled it out to length, touched the sharp blade to the skin on the top.

Escalante stared at the tiny drop of blood that appeared; a small cut.

DeMarco stared down at himself; probably it didn't look all that small to him, because he started going, "Lemme be, Jesus, lemme be, you got the wrong idea, I'm really a good guy," and as Escalante listened he remembered using some of the same words less than twenty-four hours before, in the parking lot, begging Osgood Percy not to hurt him any more "...lemme be...I'm really a good guy...lemme be...."

"You're not mad at me, then?" Holly said.

"Nuh—" He struggled in the chair but it was useless.

"Good. 'Cause I'm not mad at you either and I'm gonna give you the same break you gave me, tell me you love me and if I believe you, then you can keep it, but if I don't believe you, then you're a bad boy and bad boys must be punished, so The Envy of All Mankind will have to go away with me."

"I love you."

"I don't think that's very sincere." She turned to Escalante. "Do you think he sounds sincere?"

Escalante shook his head. "This is your show."

Holly snapped the garden shears again. "Last chance," and she looked at DeMarco.

"I fuckin' love ya, I love ya, I do, I just love . . ." He was breathing harder now. "Love . . ." Now his skin was beginning to pale. "I . . ." His voice was a whisper. "Don't, please, please, I made a mistake . . . anyone can . . ." and those were the last words that made sense because he was crying, tears of panic coming down.

Escalante looked at the giants on the floor as they watched. Bad form again by DeMarco. The worst. You didn't blubber like that, and the scorn in the giants' eyes echoed the thought, and how much would DeMarco have to pay to keep their eternal silence that he hadn't, under the pressure of a woman scorned, folded?

DeMarco fainted then, his head flopping down.

Holly hesitated not a moment. She put the shears on the desk top, stood, moved to the TV set, put her hat back on, made sure the veil was properly covering, picked up her purse.

Escalante went to the door. She moved to him, turned a moment, surveyed the wreckage. "I wish I'd brought my camera," she said, and then they were in the corridor and heading down silently in the elevator and when they hit the lobby he guided her to the nearest exit and outside into the cold night, around to her car. "Want a lift home?"

He nodded. They both got in.

She started to drive. "We make some team."

"Made some team. You can't come back here anymore."

"I know and you know what?—I don't want to shock you but there are nicer places than here, such as—"

"—don't tell me where you're headed, I don't want to know, that way I can't tell anybody."

"You that positive they'll come after you?"

"Oh, sure."

"You could have put them away."

"I try not to do that."

She hit his street, turned, slowed as she approached his apartment. "I'll call in every so often, keep tabs."

He nodded.

"You can't keep tabs on me, 'cause you won't know where I am."

"Get to it, Holly."

"Whatever do you mean?"

"You're trying to get to something in your roundabout way and pretty soon you'll be rambling on and blah-dee-blah."

She laughed. "You know me better than anybody, but you're wrong this time."

He brought out the bundle of cash. "I think it has to do with this."

"No. I told you. You're wrong. You keep it all." She stopped the car, let the motor run. "You're the one took the risk, I don't want any of it."

"Let's not end on a lie, Holly."

She looked at him in the darkness. "Okay, I want half, I'm the one took the beating."

He laughed, slipped off the rubber band. The money was in hundreds. He counted out her share. She took it, shoved it in her purse. "You'll get the other ninety thousand someday, I got faith."

He opened the car door on his side. "Stay clear of those all-black nights."

"I will." She reached out, touched his arm. "Thank you for what you did and I want you to know I never would have begged for your help if there had been more than just the three of them."

"Let's not end on a lie, Holly."

She laughed. "Okay, maybe five, you could handle five, couldn't you, Mex?"

"Not happily." He got out, closed the door, came around to her side.

"You know the craziest thing, Nikki?—Back there when he was coming apart at the seams, you know what?—I *loved* it."

She kissed him, held him awkwardly, briefly, let him go. "And I knew you when you had braces," Nick Escalante said.

# CHAPTER 3

# The Weight

His apartment, as he entered it and flicked on the light, was not as stomach-churning to him as it was ordinarily, probably because of the ten thousand dollars he held in his hand. Ten thousand couldn't make his place palatial, but at least he didn't want to turn around and flee.

It was basically one room. Basically? What kind of cow flop was that—his apartment *was* one room, no matter how much the guy who rented it to him insisted calling the area near the kitchenette a "dining alcove." The kitchenette had never been used except for storage—Escalante did not find cooking a particularly creative endeavor. Creative endeavor? —more cow flop. He hated cooking. Plus, when you lived where he lived, your best chance of having the insect population pass you by was simply not to leave food around. Escalante's refrigerator was mostly for beer, the freezer compartment for Finlandia vodka, Scotch and ice. The small stove he used for storage—valuable travel books, magazine articles that held particular interest. He had not lit the stove once in fourteen years.

The outstanding feature of his apartment was its tiny terrace. He lived on the second floor and the terrace was big enough for a couple of people to stand or one to sit and have a cool one at the end of the day. It was a pleasant thing to do, at least in theory. The realities, however, took some of the pleasure away. In the first place, the weather in Vegas was usually so hot the idea of going anywhere that wasn't air-conditioned was looney tunes. Also, the location of the terrace on a main street of Naked City made it, on occasion, dangerous. Naked City was not necessarily the worst black/Spanish slum in the state—rating slums was not an exact science. But this much was certain: You could not make a list of the half dozen worst places in all Nevada and leave Naked City off.

Escalante's terrace faced Bonanza, and there was always a lot of movement in the street, crazies, staggering bottle-throwers, gun-toting minority members who had hit bottom. Over the years, Escalante had been fired on close to half a dozen times, but none of the shots came close, the gunman almost always being too drunk to aim. Besides, if you were weaving down Bonanza in your car, as most of the violent ones did, hitting anything you aimed at wasn't easy.

The decor of his room had been a problem for him once. The landlord insisted on only using paint the color of shit brown because it didn't get dirty as quickly as some others, and there was no way shit brown upped your spirits, especially when you came home late having spent endless hours doing work not necessarily awe-inspiring. But after a little, Escalante realized his solution and it was this: maps.

Every visible brown spot was covered over with maps now. All the walls, plus some giant walking maps of the Lake District, filled most of the ceiling. It took him weeks to get the job done, but when he did, he never wanted to change anything. One place or another, all the continents were covered, dozens of countries, wonderful blue lakes and oceans, wonderful dark green marshlands, all the colors, all the roads curving across the ceiling, all the mountains to be climbed.

When he had the hundred thousand.

The five free years.

Would he ever? Absolutely. Less than three hours ago he was skulking around with his wooden Magnum protecting the uncrowned king of the weirdos, Cyrus Kinnick, the splinter with the Arafat beard, keeping the evil spirits away while Kinnick moved from hundred-dollar bet to Perrier bottle, back and forth.

Now he held ten thousand dollars cash in one hand.

He dropped the bundle onto his bed. It made a soft, comforting sound as it bounced once, lay still. He picked it up again, dropped it again.

Ninety thousand to go.

He left the money on his bed, went to his main closet—there were almost two in the apartment, the second one being so small it would have been great for Hervé Villechaize, not so great for anyone else, and began to undress. The leather jacket and slacks were of the highest quality, the gift of a now-departed pimp, not a bad fellow, considering his line of trade, and Escalante had done him something once, the clothes coming in appreciation.

He slipped off the lizard boots, put them on the floor of the Villechaize closet, removed his various rings and jewelry, the heavy gold octagon, the other chains, carefully cleaned them in the sink, dried them with a fresh towel, made sure all the blood flecks were gone, put them back in the top right drawer of his dresser.

When he was naked, he walked to the bathroom, got the shower hot, stood under it a goodly while, letting the water work at the various muscles of his back, arms and shoulders.

As he began to relax, Holly filled his thoughts, but she was gone, a sadness, true, there weren't that many gold-star girls lurking around, but it was best she was gone, best for her, anyway. And it would be best for him if he tucked her away. They were the past now, and sure, he could summon her when he felt mopey, but now was not the time.

Escalante rotated his shoulders as the water pounded down. Considering the energy he had so recently expended, the suddenness of the movements, he was in remarkably good shape. Sometimes when he dived and rolled up, if the timing wasn't perfect, there could be a soreness that lasted for days. None now. He turned the taps to cold, took it as long as he could for circulation, then back to a more comfortable temperature while he soaped and shampooed. Finished, he let the water drum against his neck muscles just for the hell of it. Then he turned off the shower, toweled dry.

He went back into the bedroom, put the stack of hundreds on his bed table, went to the freezer, got out the Finlandia, took a glass, poured himself a double, went to the bed, started to reach for something to read, instead took the money, held it in his hand. He took a vodka sip, spread the hundreds across the bedspread. As if he were playing some new kind of casino, the kind some Arab might have invented coming home in his private 747 on a dull day.

Ten rows of ten.

Jesus.

Think of what the whole hundred thousand would look like. He took another sip of Finlandia, stared at the money covering most of his bed. Then he expertly slid his hand under each row, gathered the green, made a single stack again, put the rubber band around it, dropped it onto his bed table.

It felt so goddam good. For perhaps the first time he understood how Scrooge got that way.

Ten thousand dollars.

One tenth of five years. And the rest would come. It had to. It had to.

He finished the vodka now, took the glass to the kitchenette, washed it clean, set it upside down to dry. This time when he reached his bed he grabbed *The Airline Handbook* and lay down. Pinky more often than not read books on roulette theories when he needed escapist literature. Escalante was always at ease with *The Airline Handbook.* It was a guide to sixteen hundred civil air carriers all around the world. Plus other terrific stuff, like one hundred of the most popular commercial aircraft, listing each for type and number of engines and cruise speed and range in miles and passenger seat capacity and the nationality of the manufacturer. Most of these Escalante pretty well knew. Like the Boeing 747 SP, an American pure jet, four-engined, that could carry three hundred and thirty passengers at a speed of five hundred and ninety miles per hour for a maximum distance of sixty-eight hundred miles.

Fucking poetry.

"Three-fifty-two," he said out loud, and then turned to that page in the book. Hmm. Pakistan International Airlines. Good pick. He hadn't read up on them lately. Now he started in. Established 1951. Carried three and a quarter million passengers in '82. Over twenty-one thousand employees. Routes to . . . routes to . . .

Escalante put the book on his stomach and lay staring at the maps on the ceiling, surprised momentarily. Because just then, at that moment, he couldn't have cared less where the hell Pakistan International went to.

Odd. He couldn't remember such a lack of interest before. But he felt, he felt, no question, itchy. He looked at his watch. 2:15. Hours before dawn when he could sleep.

He got up, fingers flicking against his thumbs, and went to his kitchenette, hard by the dining alcove, and another Finlandia was possible but he didn't like getting drunk, didn't do it often, especially not this early, so he settled for a cold Bud, opened it, took it back and lay down again.

Well, there was always television.

Except he hated television, every program since *The Mary Tyler Moore Show* had taken a powder and he was itchy, sure, but not desperate, at least not television desperate.

Then, thank God, he remembered the article on chronobiology that Froggie had stolen for him from a medical journal the last time he worked at the emergency ward up in Reno. Froggie said it was a good piece of elementary research and that he knew the Mex would like it. So it had been saved for a special time. Escalante got up again—"What do you do for a living?"—"Oh, I get out of bed a lot"—went to his stove, opened it, found the article quickly, lay back down.

Chronobiology is basically the study of how time affects

living organisms, and a number of people were beginning to realize the importance, for example, that jet lag had on businessmen and diplomats when they traveled east–west or vice versa. There is little jet lag when you fly north–south. Most birds fly north–south. Those few species that have an east–west journey always rest for days along the way, breaking the trip up, no jet lag for them.

Escalante stared at the maps above him, wondering how the hell birds knew that, to stop, break off for a while if they were going east or west.

Fascinating.

Incredible.

So if it was so fascinating and incredible, why did he flip the article aside and stare straight up.

Goddammit, he was itchy.

Then he realized what he needed to calm himself; he had been major league dumb not to reach right for it, and now he did, carefully bringing his wondrous Masai throwing stick close to his face, studying the dark hard wood. It was phallic, and the warriors often stood with their sticks high between their legs, stood that way for hours.

Escalante sat on his bed, closed his eyes, easily found the balance point of the weapon, began experimenting in his mind with the best kind of trajectory, how great a distance could you use if you wanted to stun an enemy, how near would you have to be to pierce his heart.

What an incredible weapon.

What a fascinating thing.

So if it was so incredible and fascinating, why did he put the throwing stick back on his bed table, stand, start to pace?

Had he ever been this itchy?

Answer: not remotely. Not ever. Not even close.

Why, though? *Why?* He sought to find the answer in the beer, chugged it, to his surprise did. He was itchy for a very legitimate reason: Tonight he was starting on his second five thousand in Las Vegas and he simply could not bear to be alone.

The Silver Spoon was the logical place. Roxy wasn't on, but the night girl, Alice Ann, knew enough to give him table seventy-five. He dressed quickly, dark socks, oxblood loafers, khakis, blue shirt, camel cardigan, then out the door, then back inside.

He wanted to take the bundle with him. Maybe Kinnick would still be betting a hundred bucks at a crap table. Escalante might walk by, nod, take out his ten thousand, let it register on Kinnick, make some chitchat, then continue on.

He had not been this flush for a while. Add in the three hundred from Osgood Percy and he had some stash in his right-hand pants pocket. If only he could earn that much each day he'd have the mythic one hundred thou at the end of the month.

It should only happen.

His mood was already better. He wasn't itchy anymore. He took his keys and turned out the lights and outside the December night was cold but to hell with it, Naked City was close to the Strip, behind it, yes, out of sight, certainly, but in the vicinity thereof. So he hotfooted it over instead of driving. There were a few cries from inside the crummy houses, drunken shouts of fear or despair, the usual night music of the area. Sometimes the anguish got to him. Usually the anguish got to him.

Not tonight, baby.

Considering it was almost Christmas and the time was twenty 'til three, the Silver Spoon was doing a business. Escalante glanced across the casino as he entered, saw Kinnick still playing craps and a gaggle of blue-haired ladies swarming around the roulette tables.

He continued on toward the coffee shop, wondering how people could piss their money away on games like that, because craps was a con, all the noise and hustle, just phony, and roulette was, if you could credit it with being anything at all, at best but a cure for insomnia, the wheel going around and around 'til your eyeballs begged for mercy.

The only game, at least from his point of view, was blackjack; it was fast, honest, it was *mano a mano,* you against the dealer, if you came closer to twenty-one than he did, you won, if you didn't, the dealer raked in the chips. If you busted and went over twenty-one, you lost, the same for him. If you tied, it was a push and you kept your chips. Square. As fair a shake as you could ask from a casino that wanted to bleed you, the only trouble being sometimes the squeals from the nearby slot machine nuts when they hit a jackpot and their machine made that goddam farting noise. Nobody, at least Escalante had yet to meet one, nobody who liked slot machines had an I.Q. above the low double figures.

Alice Ann seated him at table seventy-five, said she'd do her best with table fifty-eight. Escalante ordered coffee and looked around at all the faces. The casino was eating most of them up by this time. The fatigue lines around the eyes, the regret clear in their faces.

The coffee came, he sipped it, it tasted cruddy. He sipped again, looked at table fifty-eight, decided he wasn't in the mood just then, no matter who Alice Ann might get, so he paid, stood, left.

Ten 'til three now.

He wandered out into the casino. Somebody was having a hot run at a crap table, a lot of shouts emanating from a single area. He moved away, watched the blue-haired ladies watch the spinning roulette wheel. Cassandra (her real name) was dealing blackjack to a couple of drunks, so he moved to her table. She was his favorite dealer, young, small-handed but super-quick with the cards. Five feet tall, dark brown hair, as quick with a smile as she was with her hands. He had done her something once, a few years back, but she was in good shape now, married to a guy twice her age who ran the showroom. Escalante stopped. As Cassandra dealt, her eyes flicked to him, the smile came, went, then back to business with the drunks. They both played stupidly, busted. The same the next hand. Then, sullen, they shoved their way off the chairs and left.

"You're too tough, Cassie."

She made a muscle with her right arm, smiled, stood still, waiting. "I'm killing everyone tonight."

"How much of the shift you have left?"

She glanced at her watch. "Fifteen minutes."

Escalante moved into the nearest chair. "I'll keep you company." He got out a hundred, handed it to her.

"I warn you, Nikki—bet small."

He nodded.

"Fives okay?"

Another nod.

She reached into the chip case, took out two stacks of yellow chips, instinctively grasped ten in each hand, pushed them over. He bet a single chip, five dollars. She reached into the shoe that held the cards, gave him two cards facedown, gave herself two, one down, one up. Her up card was an ace. "I told you," she said.

Escalante looked at his cards. A four and a five. "Hit me," he said. "Big." She flipped him another down card. A three. "Again." The fourth card was a king, making a grand total of twenty-two. "Bust," Escalante said, turning his cards over. Cassie's down card was a nine. Total of twenty. Tough to beat.

He bet another five-dollar chip.

She dealt the cards quickly. He stayed at sixteen, she won with an eighteen.

The third hand he busted again.

And the fourth.

The fifth he just lost.

The sixth, another bust.

The seventh he won. Five big bucks. The next one too. It was the one after that, the ninth, that was the life-changer.

Halfway through the ninth hand, she had to reshuffle the decks. She emptied the shoe, took the four decks, set to work. Escalante looked at his cards. A ten and an eight. Eighteen. A good enough hand.

Cassie's up card was a queen.

He sat there, sat at the table, watching her small hands shuffle the cards, and as she worked he became convinced of one thing: Her down card, the one he couldn't see, was another picture. Giving her a total of twenty. Making his eighteen shit.

Except he didn't feel bad about it, didn't feel bad about anything just then, how could you, when you'd been kissed by fortune, because he'd heard of it, he'd seen it happen to others, had even felt it himself—

—but never like this, never as sudden and strong as this, there was a weight on his shoulders now, luck was riding on his shoulders now, out of all the people in all the casinos in all the world, luck had chosen to camp out with Nick Escalante.

There was no doubt in his mind. Absolutely none, and he didn't want to guess why, maybe the repayment for five thousand days, but his hands were perspiring as she finished shuffling, gave him a chance to cut the cards, which he accepted, and then she got the cards even, put them back in the shoe, burned the top card, a five, looked at him with her quick smile.

"Cassie?"

"What?"

He turned his cards over. "I've got eighteen but I know something—you've got twenty, you'll win if I stand, I *know* it."

"You sure you're okay, Nikki?"

"No. I'm great. I'm so fucking great, Cassie, believe it, and I want you to hit the eighteen."

She looked at him, hesitated, gave him a card.

It was an ace.

"Nineteen's not good enough. Hit me again. I'd like a two."

He got a two.

"Twenty-one. Turn your card over."

Another queen. "Jesus," Cassie said.

Escalante took the chips, got up from the table, walked away, or started to, because he needed time to think, what do you do when luck is so strong you can goddam *feel* it—

—you don't walk away, asshole.

He sat down at the table, took out his bundle, peeled a thousand, handed it to her. "Give me one chip, Cassie. The black."

The black was worth a thousand.

He put it in front of him. She dealt. He had nineteen, she busted. He bet two blacks. She dealt. He had fifteen, held there, she busted. He bet four thousand the next hand and when he beat her, twenty to seventeen, he had eight thousand dollars. He only bet two this time, because if she won, that way he wouldn't be back to where he'd started and—

—and *fool*! She *couldn't* win. Not with what he felt on his shoulders, he should have bet all eight, that way he'd have ended up with sixteen.

It was no contest. She busted.

Well, he had ten thousand, nothing wrong with that, not so terrible, ten thousand dollars for two minutes' work. Cassie's replacement came then, an old guy with too many rings. Escalante didn't like his eyes. He got up. "Hang in, Nikki," Cassie told him as she headed off for her break.

He reached into his pocket, got out five hundred, called her back, tipped her, then strolled to the bar for a drink, holding the ten black chips in his right hand. He ordered a Finlandia, rocks, changed his mind, decided on a club soda. He cupped both hands together, brought them to his mouth, blew warmly on the black chips. Christ. Before breakfast he had been nearly broke. Then three hundred from Osgood. Then the DeMarco ten. And now, on the night of his five thousandth morning, he had twenty thousand dollars plus in cash and blacks.

God, when luck came calling, what a thing that was—

—what the fuck, Nick Escalante thought, how do I know that it's gone? Just because a dealer shifts, just because a guy has too many rings and you don't like his eyes, that doesn't mean you aren't still on a roll.

Get away from here, get back there, *back there.*

He left the bar, returned to the casino, walked around the blackjack pit. His luck *had* changed. He could tell right off.

It was stronger.

He sat at an empty table, took out his blacks, put them in front of a young hotshot dealer. The limit at the table was five thousand. Escalante put five blacks in front of him. His stomach was taut now, his hands almost shaking, but he pressed them down hard on the green table.

The dealer busted.

He bet five again.

The dealer busted.

"Can I raise the limit?"

"No." The voice came not from the dealer but the pit boss, who was staring at him now, not bothering to disguise the way he felt. Pit bosses always took it personally when a gambler got on a roll. They hated to lose, as if it were somehow their money.

Escalante took five black chips, put them in front of him, took five more, put them on the empty place beside him.

He got two shitty hands, a fourteen and a twelve, the worst, but the dealer had a two showing and Escalante knew what he should do, hit his hands. He was not inexperienced when it came to blackjack—so he also knew that out of every hundred hands the dealer busted 28.36 times.

And this was going to be one of those times. No question about it.

The dealer busted.

He bet ten again, five thousand each on the two places, then something told him not to, so he pulled the blacks off fast, instead bet just one spot with just one chip. A yellow. Worth five bucks total.

The dealer got a twenty.

Escalante busted.

"What the fuck is this?" the pit boss said.

"Retribution," Escalante said. "And watch your mouth," Escalante said, and he bet five thousand each on two spaces, won again. His breath was coming harder now, though he tried to hide it, and he knew he'd better get the hell away, gather himself, so he stuffed all the blacks into his cardigan pockets, stood, went to the bar, ordered a Finlandia, rocks, and stared at the drink when it came.

He was up to eighty thousand dollars. He looked at his watch. 3:20. In half an hour or so he had earned seventy thousand dollars. How much was that per minute? He tried to figure, quit, who gave a shit how much it was per minute, or per second—all that mattered was the streak wasn't happening to some fat lady from Keokuk, it was all, all his.

He finished the drink in a swallow, stood, tested himself. He was under control again. The shaking was gone, the sweating definitely on the decline. He moved back to the blackjack area, conscious now how everyone who worked for the casino was keeping an eye on him.

He was twenty thousand dollars from his dream—if the luck still rode. He walked around and around the blackjack area. He wasn't sure. He didn't think the weight was gone but he wasn't that used to knowing when it was there so how could he be sure if it was gone or not?

He decided that whatever he did, he had to do it fast, in and out, don't take anything for granted, so he looked for an empty table only there wasn't one—it was getting later now and some of the blackjack pit was roped off for the night and the tables left, plenty of tables left, all had someone playing. Or two people. Or more.

Did that mean anything? Did your luck only ride you when you were alone?

He didn't know but he had to do something, and *now,* so he sat at a table with a sweet-looking elderly couple—that had to be good, no way luck would get ticked at him—and he bet the limit at this table. Three thousand.

He won.

Eighty-three.

Now he bet two places. He won. Eighty-nine. He bet three places and when he won he was at ninety-eight. He bet three places again. If he won, it was over and he had a hundred and eight thousand dollars and good-bye dear and amen.

If he lost he'd still be close to ninety, not bad for a night's work. Either way, this was the end of it. Now the nerves were back. He folded his fingers together while the dealer dealt the cards. Escalante looked at his first hand.

Twenty.

Twenty for the second.

The third was nineteen.

And the dealer had a seven showing.

The old couple did their betting. Then the dealer turned his bottom card over. A ten. Seventeen. He had to stand. "Pay eighteen, or better," the dealer said.

Escalante turned his cards over.

The pit boss said "Son of a fucking bitch" and stared at the dealer. The dealer handed over the blacks.

"Let me have a chip box," Escalante said. The dealer got one. It was plastic and had room for four rows of twenty-five chips. Escalante filled it, stuck the eight extra blacks into his cardigan pocket.

It was not until he stood that he was aware of two things: how weak his legs were and that Kinnick had been watching.

"Incredible," Kinnick said.

Escalante was about to speak but he wasn't sure he could trust his voice so he just nodded, walked past Kinnick, heading for the bar, got halfway there, realized that more than a drink he needed to *tell* someone, so he did a right turn, went to the nearest pay phone. Pinky and the Frog Prince, they were the ones. The only ones really who would truly understand. Who would care enough. Who would know that his life, at last, had entered a phase of freedom, five years of it. He dialed.

No answer at their place.

Shit. He looked at his watch. 3:32. Where the hell would they be? He could make a casino run but more than likely they weren't betting, so maybe they were out eating but who knew at which armpit?

He dialed again, because maybe he'd screwed it up the first time, what with his hands shaky and all.

No answer at their place.

Slowly he put the phone back, waiting for what he had always known would happen, for the sudden exhilaration to knock him sideways.

Too nervous yet. Nothing had sunk in yet. His legs were still weak, his hands trembling. He stared at the chip box and the hundred black beauties in their four perfect rows. Not to mention their eight brothers in the cardigan. Not to mention the ten thousand in his pants pockets.

Jesus, Jesus.

"Can I buy you a drink?"

Escalante turned. It was Kinnick, Arafat beard and all. "No."

"Oh, sorry, no intrusion meant," and Kinnick began to retreat.

"Hey, time out, I didn't mean I wouldn't drink with you,

I meant a man wins a hundred thousand plus, he's got to be the one doing the buying. Okay? Let me buy *you* a drink."

"It would be my pleasure." They started toward the closest bar.

"What do people call you?"

"Cyrus *is* a shitty name, if that's your implication, and you're right. I always wanted to be called 'Ace' or 'Duke,' but 'Cyrus' is the overwhelming choice."

Escalante nodded, they moved to a table, sat. "Perrier?" Escalante said.

"Finlandia vodka on the rocks with a twist," Kinnick said. "I'm not going to gamble much more, it doesn't matter if my head's clear or not."

Escalante ordered two doubles when the waitress came.

"You don't seem as excited as I would be, this happen before?"

"Never close." He shook his head. "You're right, I'm not as excited as I thought I'd be either, I'm thinking too much is why, I should just ride with it, but I can't turn off my brain. I mean, you wouldn't guess what's going on inside."

The drinks came. Escalante paid. Kinnick held his glass out, they clinked glasses. "Whatever you've got going tonight, may some of it please rub off on me."

They drank on that.

Escalante started laughing then. "It's crazy, but see, I've got a storage space out on Mojave, it's open twenty-four hours, and all I keep thinking is what should I put there when I cash in and go pack at my place tonight? What should I save?"

"You're leaving town?"

"Think bigger. State, country, continent, you name it, I'm gone. That's what this means"—he held up the chip case—"Five years, Duke—five free years, and all for me. I told myself I'd get it someday but probably I never really thought it would happen. That's why I'm not excited now—I can't stop to enjoy it, I just want to fly. Whatever the first plane is in the morning, no matter how early it leaves, wherever it goes, I'm on it."

"I take it you haven't loved living here all that much."

"Doesn't matter now. Not anymore." He stared at the hundred chips in their perfect rows. Goddam Pinky—where the hell did he and the Frog Prince go? Not that there was anything wrong with Kinnick, probably a decent enough weirdo, but Kinnick couldn't share this with him, Kinnick could try but that was all. And it wasn't enough. He excused himself, went back to the phone, dialed Pinky again, and shit—no answer, just the buzzing going on forever. He hung up, returned to the bar, and his stomach was tense again, or at least starting to get that way as Kinnick said, "Can I at least offer to buy the next round?"

"No next round." Escalante finished his drink quickly.

Kinnick did the same. "Maybe I'll give the crap tables one last chance. Good-bye—it hasn't been the evening I expected, but I won't forget it, either." He stood, walked away, in his perfectly tailored Ivy League clothing with the pistol that was probably loaded safe in the shoulder holster.

Escalante sat a moment longer, looked around the Silver Spoon, wondered how many hours he had sat in the coffee shop, and was there anything else about the place aside from table seventy-five he might miss.

Nope.

He got up. He felt funny. He sat down. Itchy again. Like back in his room. His stomach was knotting, his hands were unsteady. He considered another drink, decided against it, stood, made his slow way, clutching the chip case in his hands, and across the casino was the cage where the money was and all he had to decide was how he wanted his winnings returned, hundreds or thousands or what, and that should have been an easy decision, because the truth was, it didn't matter, just so it all added up to the same total, he could take it in pennies and who cared, and now the cashier's cage was twenty steps away and now ten and then he was there and as he began to hand over the chip case, just the most terrible thing happened to him, just the worst-ever thought crossed his mind and for a moment, he was actually afraid the power of the realization was going to make him fall helpless to the casino floor—

—because, he realized, the dream that had sustained him, the wish for the freeing one hundred thousand, the ensuing travel and never resting his head twice on the same pillow—

—all, all horseshit, all a loser's dream.

Because the truth was, and he stood frozen as nearby a woman began to shriek as her slot machine registered a jackpot, the truth was this: A hundred thousand dollars was nothing.

No.

Worse.

It was torment.

Yes, the first year would be thrilling. But halfway through the second year it would dawn that in just one year more he would be halfway through his dream, and each day from then on would become increasingly more frantic, more tormenting, because each day would bring him not pleasure but the sure pain that the return to this place would bring.

"Do you want something, sir?" The girl cashier was looking at him.

"Yes," he managed.

"What?"

"I don't—I don't even know," Nick Escalante said, and he turned from the cage, and Pinky would be able to help him, the Frog Prince would be reasonable, so he called them again and there was just the sound of the phone buzzing implacably.

He went to the keno area because it was closest and sat huddled with his winnings in his hands. What *did* he need? All these years he had told himself that what he needed was what he held, one hundred thousand, but he had never had one hundred thousand before, so he had never pressed his logic, the amount seemed so inconceivable.

What *did* he need?

He closed his eyes, thinking of rivers and cities and mountains and skies, and then he opened his eyes and stared around at the innards of the windowless clockless casino and what he needed, at last, he realized was this—

—fuck-you money.

Enough money so that he would *never* have to return. Fuck-you money would buy him the only thing that really mattered: freedom, lasting and eternal.

How much, though? He was never into finance, never in his life had bought or sold a piece of stock, but he had heard of those things, bonds, what were they called, he couldn't quite get it, tax-free somethings, yes, wait, tax-free municipals, and what did they pay, ten percent? No, less, eight, more likely. Eight percent. Now he took a pencil and a keno pad and tried to figure how much he would have to have in order to earn twenty thousand a year forever.

It wasn't hard, actually. One hundred thousand at eight percent got you eight thousand dollars a year tax-free. Double that, and you had sixteen thousand a year tax-free. Half of eight was four thousand, bringing it up to the needed twenty. Twenty a year tax-free.

To get that he needed two hundred and fifty thousand dollars.

That was fuck-you money. That was freedom. And he had one hundred and eight in chips and ten in cash. Almost halfway there. Probably he could invest that amount, Pinky would know how, carefully invest it and in another five, six, seven years, he'd have what he needed.

Except he couldn't last another five, six, seven years, he knew it. Then he knew something else, felt the weight almost perceptibly on his shoulders: Luck was still riding with him. He looked at his watch. 3:55. He glanced around.

Cassie was back at her blackjack table. He walked over, said nothing, just put one black chip from his cardigan pocket on the table. She dealt. He had eighteen. She had a blackjack.

That was good. Couldn't have been better. One blackjack out of her system. "I want to play the whole table, Cassie. All seven spots."

She looked at him.

"And I don't want any limit."

"I'll have to clear that."

"Clear it."

She moved, whispered to the pit boss, who scowled at Escalante, then nodded his okay. Cassie came back. "You're on."

He took the remaining seven black chips from his pocket, put one at each spot. She dealt. He got good cards. She got another blackjack. "I told you, Nikki, I'm a killer."

"You're a pussycat. Believe me." He began to feel the exhilaration now. The luck was riding so strong. She had two blackjacks gone now. And the weight of luck on his shoulders was better than any caress he had ever had from any woman. Almost any woman. It was a wondrous weight. He wished it there forever as he opened his chip case. One hundred black beauties. He started small, a thousand per spot.

She busted.

He doubled.

He busted.

Back to a thousand per spot. He won five, lost two. He went up to three thousand per spot. Twenty-one thousand on the table as the pit boss moved in beside Cassie. Her top card was bad for her—a six. He made sure he didn't bust because he knew for damn sure that she would.

She did.

He looked at his watch. Three minutes after four. And he was up to—for a moment he tried to figure but to hell with it—he was hovering around one-two-five—

—halfway.

"Let me have another chip case, Cassie."

She nodded, got him one. He took his time—there was no shaking in his hands now—filling the first back up, starting in on the second. He didn't feel lucky this hand so he dropped down to a chip a spot.

She lucked into a twenty-one.

Escalante smiled as she took the chips. Because he could still read the cards. Luck was his lover still. And now the weight was heavy. He had never come close to betting this much but he took a breath, put five chips on each spot. Thirty-five thousand.

She busted.

"I'm changing dealers," the pit boss said.

"You do and I quit. And you don't want me betting someplace else because you think I'll go cold, don't you?"

"I'm changing cards, then."

"Hey, you can change underwear, asshole—which isn't a bad idea if you don't mind the hint—" He took his money, began to fill the second chip box. Closing in on one-sixty. Cassie opened the four new decks, began the labor of getting the cards ready for the shoe.

"I'm going for a drink," Escalante said. "Cassie, you watch my stuff, okay?"

She nodded. He pushed the chip boxes toward her, went to the bar, ordered a double Finlandia, rocks, a twist, downed it, thought he caught a glimpse of Kinnick sitting alone at the bar, paid, went back to the table.

Cassie burned the top card.

Escalante hesitated, didn't quite feel the luck as heavy, bet only one chip, lost, felt the same way the next deal, lost seven thousand more.

Then it was back, heavier than it had yet been, so he went very big, ten chips per spot, seventy thousand on the table. He got okay cards but he didn't feel nervous. What he felt like was what happened back in DeMarco's suite when the cry of victory escaped, because she was going to bust, Cassie was.

She did.

"Another chip box, please," Escalante said. Cassie got him one. He was over two hundred now. He looked at his watch. 4:12. He decided to count carefully what he had so he'd know what he needed. But his throat was dry. He asked Cassie to keep an eye out, hurried to the bar, ordered a glass of water, drained it, another, drained that, then a double Finlandia, rocks, twist, took that pretty fast, too, before returning to the table.

He had a crowd now. Maybe twenty people watching the chip boxes, muttering to themselves, Kinnick craning at the rear of the crowd. He sat, smiled at Cassie, counted the blacks.

Two hundred and seventeen thousand dollars. He didn't like the odd-sounding numbers so he bet three thousand total and won.

Two-twenty sounded so much better.

Now the question was simple: draw it out or go quick for eternity. Speed had its pluses, but, and he hated to admit this, he loved sitting there, knowing all those people were behind him, watching him, wanting just a touch of what he had.

He bet five thousand on one spot.

She beat him.

He bet ten thousand.

She beat him.

Two-oh-five.

Escalante looked at her. "Why you being so mean?"

She shrugged.

He took five black chips, handed them over to Cassie as a tip. Then he turned to the pit boss. "She won't be mean anymore." He was down to an even two hundred thousand now, and some part of him said to go for the bundle, bet fifty on one spot and if he won, kiss them all good-bye. He hesitated, because the weight on his shoulder was there, the luck was still there, but it had been heavier so he bet ten instead and beat her, nineteen to eighteen.

The next bet was another ten and they pushed at seventeen.

He doubled, bet twenty, beat her and now he was up to two-thirty.

His fuck-you money was twenty thousand away. Cause for celebration, certainly, not the final one, but still, you couldn't feel bad about a night like this—

—except Escalante wasn't sure the weight was still there, there on his shoulder. Should he go for it all now and bet twenty? If he won it was over, but if he lost, he was back to two-ten, a long hill to climb if your luck was leaving.

He bet ten, won, two-forty now, didn't hesitate, bet ten, lost, two-thirty, another ten, another victory, two-forty—bet ten for eternity, lost, shit, back to two-thirty, they were seesawing, him and Cassie, and he had to break the rhythm, but did he dare, not quite, he bet ten, she busted, he was at two-forty for the God knows what time, and now he felt the weight again, decided to break the chain, bet twenty, he'd have two-sixty if he won, two-twenty if he didn't, not so terrible, at least he didn't think it would be until he busted and the pit boss let him have a smile and that really pissed Escalante, so he bet fifty, pulled the bet back because he was angry now and you did stupid things when you tried to bet angry so he got up again, pushed his boxes to Cassie, had his glass of water, his Finlandia, rocks, twist, then back and it was a good break, the pit boss could smile all he wanted, Escalante was in control, and he bet fifty, took the loss without a twitch, because the weight was still with him, and he did a little figuring, looked at his watch, 4:19, and he counted out forty-five black chips, bet it on one spot, drew a nineteen, watched as she had a six and a six and a three and a five for her twenty, beating him.

"Okay," Nick Escalante said.

"Done?" Cassie asked.

"Just revving up." He pushed the chip boxes over. "That's a hundred and twenty-five thousand dollars, count it."

She clocked the five rows of chips.

"Let's go."

"You sure, Nikki?"

"It's half of two-fifty, what's the big deal?" She gave him two cards. A seven and a ten. And her up card was a king. He stared at her, then at her hole card. He had rarely felt as calm. He knew, as he had known once already this evening, that her hole card was another ten, so what he needed, ideally, was a four, and he'd like that right off, avoid the wait, but he wouldn't mind an ace and a three or a two and another two, just so the total reached twenty-one, and when he said "Hit me" he thought for a moment that he might have made a mistake, something, the look in her eyes, the way her shoulders seemed almost to sag as she flipped him the eight, busting him, turned over her hole card, a five, if he'd sat on his seventeen, she'd have been the one busting, and for a moment he wondered when that impact would hit but then he thought, fuck that, that's not important, what was important was he still had ten thousand left, DeMarco's cash, and he pulled the wad from his pocket, bet it all, got a twenty, good but not enough to handle her blackjack and then he was at the bar, drinking another Finlandia, rocks, twist, a triple this time, and another, but when he reached for his money to pay, it turned out he didn't have any but that took a while to find out because his hand couldn't locate his pocket and his legs were wobbling, and he tried reaching for the barstool, missed, spun, fell hard facedown on the floor, got up, or started to, but his arms wouldn't hold him for long enough, and before he fell again all he could see was something red on the bar floor, blood on the bar floor, his. . . .

# CHAPTER 4
# The Gift

Mornings were never easy for him.

But this, the five thousand and first, was the most torturous of all. Escalante blinked, knew from habit the time, ten in the morning, flicked through the day ahead, saw not a great deal that he could hold tight to. No. There would be nothing for him but the constant replaying of his behavior at the blackjack table.

He knew he had to try to go someplace, and he'd had a Hollywood agent once, a good client and a great traveler who said no place was the equal of Venice but you had to be there in the winter, risk the fog and the floods, ignore the damp, because the city was empty then, you could truly see it then, so Escalante went to Venice, and a good place to start might be Harry's Bar, have the risotto in champagne sauce, then stroll in the afternoon light through the Piazza San Marco, study the Doges' Palace, take the elevator up to the top of the Campanile, stare out at the Grand Canal, the palaces, with the Lido off in the distance, the islands named . . . named . . .

. . . no good.

His mind would not function. His head hurt too much for that. It was also hard to breathe. He opened his eyes slowly, wondered where he was. In a bed, certainly, but whose and how did he get there? He touched his nose. Dried blood. The table alongside had matches and an ashtray, both of them with the word "Grand" on them, so probably, no, absolutely without question, he was in a bed in a room in a suite in the Grand Hotel.

He put his feet on the floor. His clothes were still on. He

found the bathroom, looked at his face. No real damage. He got a washcloth, turned on the cool water, scraped the dried blood from his nose. It wasn't really swollen. He must have fallen on it.

When?

After he'd left the blackjack table. That must have been when. In the bar of the Silver Spoon most likely. Then the face of the pit boss came clear, smiling as he bet the last of his cash, and Escalante whirled and shut his eyes to make the vision leave.

Mistake.

He was not ready for quick movements, especially with his eyes closed. He lost his balance, slammed against the bathroom door. "Every day in every way I am getting better and better," Nick Escalante said then, walking slowly out of the bathroom, through the bedroom, opening the door, looking out into the main room of the suite.

Kinnick, stroking his Arafat beard, sat at a table, sipping coffee. He was dressed impeccably in a different Ivy League costume now, light grey slacks, navy blazer, white button-down shirt, striped tie. He looked up at Escalante. "Would you like your grapefruit juice now?"

Escalante stared at him. "How'd I get here?"

"I hope you're not upset. I didn't feel it decent to leave you lying on the floor of the bar and you didn't seem capable of much movement on your own. And I didn't know where you lived, so I tipped a couple of gentlemen to escort you to a cab and we rode for a minute and when I got to the hotel, some other staff were helpful in getting you up here, it's the only place I could think to take you, would you like your grapefruit juice now, it's chilled." He reached for a tray, lifted a large glass.

Escalante mumbled "Thank you," tried to sip the juice, but his throat was so dry and the taste was so delicious he could do nothing but chug it down.

"Shall I order you another?" Kinnick sat as before, looking up, as always, nervous or frightened or whatever.

"No, thanks. You slept on the couch?"

Kinnick nodded.

"It's your suite but you gave me the bed."

"I thought you needed a good rest more than I did. Did you have one?"

"I slept wonderfully, thank you."

"That's good."

Escalante looked at the skinny kid. More nervous now than ever.

"Duke—you're very solicitous, you've been very helpful, I genuinely appreciate everything you've done—"

"—Oh, I forgot," Kinnick said then, getting up, hurrying over, shoving a hundred dollars into Escalante's hand. "I forgot to pay you, for last night, you left so quickly and I don't like owing people."

Escalante stared at the money. "I ditched you, what the hell are you paying me for?"

"For your time—and I won't take it back, not a penny of it, so don't try and make me."

The kid was back at the table now, his hands locked together to keep the trembling hidden. Or try to.

Escalante sat in a chair across the room. "Okay," he said. "I think you have something to say and I think it's time you said it. Because I don't think it's a coincidence that we're together—in this room, sure, I happened to get drunk last night, you were there, you brought me here. But I don't think we met in Las Vegas entirely by accident."

Kinnick nodded.

Escalante rubbed his eyes, waiting.

"You won't laugh?"

"In my present mood, doubtful."

Kinnick let his hands go. The fingers drummed the tabletop. "This is . . . it's very important to me."

Escalante nodded.

"And . . . I don't want you turning me down, I've come too far for a 'no' answer."

Escalante waited, wondering if he'd ever seen as frightened a young man as the one with him now. He couldn't have. If he had, he would have remembered him, as he would remember Kinnick now, sitting there, gaunt, frail, the fingers flying in a rhythm of their own making.

"I want to be with you," Kinnick said then, and then, before Escalante could reply, he cried out, "Not like that, not in the biblical sense, Jesus, I got it wrong, I'm sorry, I'm sorry, I want to be around you. I want you to teach me."

"Teach you what?"

Kinnick hesitated. "I know who you are. I spent a lot of money finding out. I told you once, I'm very cautious. I know everything. I knew about the grapefruit juice in the morning, didn't I? And the Finlandia? Well, that's nothing."

"Teach you what? Take it easy. Nobody can help you if you won't say what you want."

"Okay—I was back in Boston and I was walking along—this won't sound like it makes sense but it does, at least it does to me—I saw this guy, this old guy, with a knapsack on his back and he was moving his arms in an . . . an almost mechanical way, so naturally, he drew attention. And on the sack, printed on the back of it, was a sign and the sign said, I'll never forget this: 'Please don't hit me.' And when I read that I thought, 'What a weird thing,' and then I realized, no it wasn't, because something about that man angered me—*I wanted to hit him*—but I couldn't, I didn't know how." Kinnick got up then, began to pace. "If I'm going to be honest, I may as well tell you this: On the phone when I said another client had recommended you, that wasn't true."

"Well, you fooled me. What do you mean you didn't know how?"

Kinnick took off his blazer, draped it over the chair, the

holster making a loud sound. He blushed. "I carry a gun," he said.

"You do?"

"Almost all the time, but I don't know why, it doesn't help." He moved to Escalante, pulled the shirt-sleeve up slightly. "Touch my wrist. Grab it."

Escalante did.

"It's a twig, isn't it, don't lie. Back in school, I was always terrified, especially during recess, because I'm like that old man with the knapsack—people were always hurting me because they knew I was too weak to defend myself. I could only do that in class. By being smarter than anybody. And you see, when I saw that old man I realized I was going to be like him someday, when I got old. Afraid, maybe crazy, wearing a sign for protection. That day I started on my search. I went to physical places, gyms, self-defense centers, and you, your name kept coming up, not all the time obviously, but more than anyone else's and then I got my hands on the interview in the magazine where the man said you were lethal, and I checked you out carefully, because this means a great deal to me as I'm sure you've gathered—I want you to teach me what you know, I want to learn it all, I want you to kill the fear that I live with every day of my life."

Escalante sagged back in the chair. "Listen, kid—"

"—I earned seven million dollars on my twenty-eighth birthday, don't call me 'kid'—"

"—Jesus, how?"

Kinnick shrugged. "It was nothing, the same way everybody does nowadays, I came up with a new twist on an old twist on computer software, I started in a garage when I was twenty-three, I sold out five years later, I hated it. No. Me. I hated me. I'll pay you for teaching me, I'll overpay you, I can make you rich."

"I've been rich, last night most recently."

"I can help you with that too."

"Help me with what?"

"Don't play games with me, I'm being honest with you." And now his voice began to get loud. "I know about addicts. Both my fucking folks were addicts and the only reason I wish they were alive is so I could kill them, it was shit with folks like that, agony, growing up afraid, with a father who gambled and a mother who drank."

"I'm not an addict."

"Are you serious?"

"I like blackjack maybe more than I should, but that doesn't mean I have a problem. I never had a night like that before in my life—I never once got so much as fifty thousand ahead, never in all these years—last night must have given you the wrong idea, because I acted crazy."

Kinnick's blue eyes stayed on him. "Surely you must realize you're a compulsive gambler."

"What are you, the word from on high? When did you get anointed?"

"I didn't mean to upset you—"

"—good—'cause you're not—"

"—but it's all so clear to me—"

"—if it's all so fucking clear, why are you so fucking wrong?—"

"—please. Try and stay calm. Look at the facts—why do you think you stay here?—you hate it so much it's the only place you *can* stay—it's the only place you're worthy of, Jesus, it's obvious, but even if you don't see it, I can make you see it, I'll help you and you help me, so say yes, I want to be you—"

"—do you know how lunatic that sounds? You're not even thirty, you're set for life, I'm staring at forty, I'm worth, counting what you just gave me, less than five hundred dollars and I'm working on a hangover that would drop Arnold Schwarzenegger, who in the world would want that?"

"I would. More than anything."

Escalante got up. It was getting too weird for him to deal with, and he'd almost had eternity in his hands six hours before when luck had found another shoulder to ride, and he knew where he had to go to feel better, the one place, the only place, so he crossed the floor and Kinnick said, "Tell me yes."

"Ace, Duke, listen, I earned my past, you'll have to earn your own."

"Tell me you'll think about it. Please, Jesus, at least tell me that."

Escalante looked at the skinny panicked weirdo with the Arafat beard. "I don't know. Maybe I'll think about it but I can't think about it *now.*" And then his hand was on the knob and he was out the door in the hallway and he turned to close the door, saw Kinnick looking about to cry. . . .

On those occasions when he was so far down he had to stare straight up with a telescope even to hope to catch a glimpse of rock bottom, there was but a single place that provided salvation, and he went there now, as fast as he could drive, not bothering to change clothes or shave or do any damn thing but *go.*

Straight to 1775 East Tropicana.

He parked, went inside, paid the three-fifty admission fee, took a deep breath and looked around, secure in the absolute knowledge that he was standing in the most symbolically perfect building ever conceived of by the mind of man.

If you asked everyone who visited Nevada what the most popular tourist attraction in the state was, the answer would come quick and easy and it would be correct: gambling. And if you asked what the second most popular attraction was, probably a fair share would come up with, again correctly, the Hoover Dam.

But very few would be able to name the third most popular tourist attraction, and Escalante stood in the center of it now, as close as he could come just then to bliss, for that was the effect that the Liberace Museum always had on him.

The Liberace Museum. An entire fucking edifice that did nothing more or less than house a career's worth of artifacts belonging to none other than Lee Liberace himself. Escalante wandered to the gift counter, studied the items on display.

God, the abundance of it all. If he'd wanted, he could have bought a miniature black baby grand piano with Liberace's very own flourished signature reproduced across the top ($24.50). Or a Liberace candy dish. Or ashtray. Or a *George* Liberace ashtray (complete with embossed violin, $3.50). Where else in the world could you buy a Liberace pillbox, a Liberace paperweight or—*or*—three bars of Liberace sandalwood-scented soap in the shape of a piano for just fifteen dollars? Was there a better bargain in any bazaar in Asia? Not just soap. Not just scented soap. But soap shaped like a fucking piano. Empires fell for less.

Already, he could feel his hangover loosen its hold. He left the gift counter to study the automobiles. A Rolls-Royce, nothing so special about a Rolls-Royce, except this one was beautifully painted in alternating red, white and blue stripes. A bat-winged Bradley GT in a tasteful metallic gold. A 1964 Cadillac limousine custom Durham, one of only two ever made. And Escalante's personal favorite, a 1956 London cab painted in a delicate black and white houndstooth.

Oh, and the pianos: great bulky things that Chopin might have played, another one where Liszt's fingers reputedly wandered.

And the glorious portrait of the great man himself, with eyes that followed you as you walked past it. Escalante moved back and forth in front of the painting, feeling for all the world like a very large child.

But nothing, not the cars or the instruments, could compete with the magic of the costumes. Escalante stood and stared at the rows of perfectly fitting fabric. There was the coat in the style of Czar Nicholas's royal uniform with braiding in twenty-two-carat gold. And next to it hung the velvet cape patterned after the coronation robes of King George V—a nice enough cape made just a little nicer by virtue of the fact that it was covered with sixty *thousand* dollars' worth of chinchilla.

Heaven.

Escalante shook his head, almost smiled, glanced around the museum. Two men stood by the door now, flanking it, watching him. They worked for Baby. A moment later, Baby himself entered. Baby glanced around, gestured for the men to leave, smiled his wondrous smile and began to cross toward Escalante.

Baby was the best and the brightest. Tall, soft-spoken, never angry, always in control. If it was possible to dress with taste when your style of attire was California Casual, then Baby was always impeccably turned out. He resembled Alan Alda, the same instant affability. If you spent an evening with him, and were told the next day that you had spent the previous night with the man who controlled the Combination in most of Nevada, you would not have considered it possible.

Baby had known Escalante for well over a decade, ever since he had unsuccessfully tried to recruit him. And whenever they came in contact with one another, it was always pleasant.

"Nicholas, Nicholas," Baby said, holding out his hand.

Escalante nodded. They shook.

"Pinky said you'd probably be here if you weren't at the Silver Spoon. I didn't know you were into serious culture."

"I only come here on special occasions. It's irresistible."

Baby smiled. "I'll give it 'unique.'"

Escalante nodded.

"Nicholas, Nicholas," Baby said.

Escalante said nothing. Whatever reason Baby had for

coming, he was more than capable of verbalizing it when he wanted.

"I hear you almost broke the bank at the Spoon last night."

"Good news travels fast, Baby."

"Christ—remember, when was it, two months ago, when you had us beat for eighty thousand at The Croesus 'til your luck changed?"

"I'll get there someday," Escalante said.

Baby looked straight at him then. "I hope so. I surely hope so. Yesterday I thought you'd live forever. Now I'm not so sure."

"Meaning?"

Baby put an arm around Escalante's shoulder, and they began walking around the perimeter of the Liberace Museum, passing hundreds of photographs, postcards, paintings. "Oh, Nicholas, I'm in a terrible bind. A terrible terrible bind. And all because of you."

Escalante waited.

"Somebody busted up 3506 at The Croesus and tied three people and took twenty thousand dollars."

"And that was before I had my Wheaties," Escalante said.

Baby broke out laughing. He had a wonderful laugh, and he held it for a long time before he said, "Oh, Nicholas, if only it was funny." Now he stopped. "You see, that same somebody also shot and killed two blond gentlemen named Tiel and Kinlaw, shot them while they were helpless. An eyewitness claims that somebody to be you."

Escalante shoved Baby's arm away. *"And you believe that?"*

"If I did you'd be dead, we both agree on that, don't we, Nicholas?"

Escalante nodded.

"I don't know, Nicholas. I truly do not know. I've known Danny DeMarco forever. His father and my father were intimate. Why would he lie? I keep asking myself. And I get no answer. He's an arrogant turd, but he's never been a liar." He shook his head. "Come along."

"To where?"

"To see DeMarco. I have to find the truth, Nicholas."

"What do you mean, I'm on trial?"

"For your life I should think," Baby said.

"Why do I have to tell it again?" Danny DeMarco said, his voice thick, his mouth still swollen from the night before. He was seated alongside Baby in Baby's office in the rear of The Croesus Hotel. The room was large, decorated quietly, muted desert colors. Escalante sat across from them in a leather chair. Behind him were several men, armed. "I told you everything, Baby. It's all true and you believe me. So why this?"

"Because, Daniel, you're asking me to kill this gentleman here, and I've known Nicholas for a long while, and it would be a dreadful thing if a mistake was made. A miscarriage would haunt me. I think he has the right to know precisely what we're accusing him of."

"Okay, okay," DeMarco said. "It's just, well, I never saw nothing like it before and thinking about it, it makes you emotional."

"I understand. Be as concise as you like. Now, please." Baby gestured for DeMarco to start.

Escalante sat very still, his fingertips touching his chin, wondering why DeMarco had shot his two guards. Was it because he had lied and said they were Holly's violators? Possible but unlikely. The reason must have been that they had seen him cry, crumble, the coward revealed, and he was much too macho a little shit to let people live with that kind of information on him. If they talked, and they would, it was too juicy to sit on forever, it would not do much for his cause as the coming king of Lexington, Kentucky.

"I guess maybe what I feel most terrible about was I let him in," DeMarco said. "See, we'd ordered food up from room service—we were having a great time, old Tiel and me, kidding Kinlaw, playing a little cards, drinking a little Scotch. And I thought the room service was pretty goddam efficient getting there so fast, so without even thinking I open the door and there this guy is standing, wearing like a pimp outfit, dark leather."

Escalante nodded.

"And he's got this bandana covering his face and a gun and he backs me in, pistol-whips me across the mouth—" DeMarco pointed to his face, to the dried red cuts on both sides of his mouth. "See?"

Baby said he did.

"He's very quick, this prick here, and he clobbers Tiel and Kinlaw bad, and then he ties them up, back to back, like they were when you found them, and he ties me to a chair. Only I'm faking like I'm out, because when he tied them up the bandana slipped and I get a glimpse of his spick face and you don't forget a face like that, not if you're into sports, he looks too much like a younger version of the guy over at Caesars, Gonzales. He rifles my desk, takes the twenty grand and then, I don't know, maybe he's pissed it ain't more, who can say, he goes crazy, goes over to my friends, takes out one of their guns, uses it while they're helpless and just like that these two guys I'd been laughing and kidding with a couple minutes earlier are gone and I'm only here because there was a noise in the corridor then, and he panicked and took off. If he'd known I'd seen his face, I'm gone, too, I know that for sure. He killed them with one of their own guns—you check, Baby, you'll see, they'll have his fingerprints all over them."

"Don't bother to check," Escalante said. "The fingerprints are mine."

"This is all true, then, Nicholas?"

"Some."

"Which?"

Escalante sat there.

"Please, Nicholas," Baby said. "It would be best, I think, if you have anything to say, to say it now. And quickly."

Escalante closed his eyes. Even if he tried to defend

himself, would it work? Baby almost had to side with DeMarco. You didn't break up the Combination. At least if he was quiet, he wouldn't have tried to win and gone out losing.

And he was so goddam tired. And he saw the black chips in the boxes, hundreds of thousand-dollar chips, and probably he shouldn't have lied to Kinnick, he was a compulsive, a trapped compulsive, everything Kinnick said was true, it was just hard to accept it right off coming from a stranger, you had to deny charges like that, that went that deep.

And even if he did convince Baby, DeMarco would do something, hire professionals for vengeance, and probably Holly wasn't safe, not anymore, DeMarco knew who he was, if he wanted he could check and find out who his friends were and did it truly make any difference, living or dying in Vegas, today or a thousand days on?

He opened his eyes then and looked at Baby. Baby was solemn. Now Escalante looked at DeMarco. DeMarco was smiling. And that was wrong. People like DeMarco should not be allowed to smile. Or win. Or any other thing. Even if he failed, Escalante knew that at the very least, he had to try and stop that smile.

Very quietly he said, "I'll just ask two questions, Baby. If you can come up with answers that satisfy you, do what you will."

Baby nodded.

"Why would I use a gun?"

"What the fuck kind of question is that?" DeMarco said. "Why does anybody use a gun?—"

"—Nicholas doesn't," Baby said softly. "Edged weapons are his specialty." He picked up a glass ashtray. "Nicholas could kill you with this, take my word. From fifteen feet away or from five." He put the ashtray down. "And I'll answer your question—you used a gun because it was a perfect piece of cover—no one would ever dream that Nick Escalante needed a piece to accomplish a robbery."

DeMarco smiled again, nodded.

"Your second question, Nicholas, please. Your second and last."

"Let me just repeat a few things, all right?"

"Of course," Baby said.

"I broke in the suite, clobbered DeMarco, tied everybody up, took the money, killed the other two and while I did, DeMarco recognized me because my bandana slipped. He was faking being unconscious but he wasn't. He was alert the whole time."

"That's right," DeMarco said.

Escalante looked at Baby. "What do you know about my body," he asked.

"I don't quite get you."

"Underneath my clothes, what do you know?"

"Obviously nothing."

"Well, then, here's my second question: How is it possible that I know that Mr. DeMarco here has a small but definitely visible cut on the upper side of his penis? I'll give you the answer: I saw it put there by a lady with a pair of garden shears in her delicate hands."

"What *is* this?" DeMarco said.

"Baby, I suspect DeMarco did in his two dear friends himself. But I don't know because I wasn't there—what I do know is that he was less than gentlemanly to a person of my acquaintance and I helped her get her own back. And that's all I did. It's very easy to find out if I'm lying: All he has to do is take his pants down."

DeMarco stood, looked at Baby. "You're not buying this crock?"

Baby was silent.

"Somebody get a microscope," Escalante said. "We'll need it to locate Mr. DeMarco's pecker."

DeMarco's voice began to rise. "I'm not stripping for this son of a bitch."

"I think you have to, Daniel," Baby said. "A man is

risking his life on a very considerable long shot. The least we can do is give him his chance. I know it's embarrassing but I'll make it easier—you and I can go into the next room. We'll both take down our trousers, fair?"

"I won't do it!"

"I think you must."

"I won't—it's a matter of principle."

Escalante had to laugh.

"*Principle,* goddammit," DeMarco repeated. "Shut him up."

Baby sighed. "Danny, you just lost—nobody in your family has had the least acquaintance with a principle in fifty years. Now, for the last time, will you go with me into the next room?"

"Fuck, no—and how can you believe this guy over me and how's my father going to take that news, do you think?"

"Here is what I think happened. I think someone who *resembles* Nicholas, here, did the shooting. And I will try very hard to find out who it is. And you may go." Baby gestured toward the door.

In a moment, Baby and Escalante were alone. "You know this isn't over," Baby said then.

"Hasn't started."

Baby nodded. "He'll hire someone to come for you. I'll pass the word here and in Reno that I'm very much against it. That should lower the quality of the opposition somewhat."

"Appreciated."

"But I'm not that strong in Tahoe."

"The Glider, you mean?"

Baby nodded. "If I were DeMarco, that's the man I'd hire."

"Don't worry about The Glider—I did him something once, several times."

"Let's hope it's enough." He stood, moved to Escalante, shook his hand, walked him to the office door. "I didn't much want to kill you."

"I know."

"You think he did it?"

"Of course."

"Why?"

"He's a very macho little slime. And he humiliated himself in front of them."

Baby shook his head. "What a wonderful reason for a double murder." He opened the office door. "You know, this is a terrible thing to admit for someone in my line of endeavor, but toughness is something the world could do with less of."

Escalante nodded. "You know what the most murderous edged weapon has always been?"

Baby didn't.

"The tongue," Nick Escalante said.

His phone was ringing when he walked into his room, which always surprised him, because so few people had been given his number. Pinky and the Frog Prince, Holly and the Paxtons, not many others.

It was Darryl. Stammering. "Can I—would it be all right if—there's a matter that's come up. Suddenly. May I come see you?"

"I'll be waiting," Escalante said, and by the time he'd shaved, showered, changed, Paxton was at the door. Escalante let him in.

Paxton held out an envelope. "It's another one—only this wasn't from L.A.—it was left in my mailbox and I didn't want Ashley to know."

"You want me to open it?"

"I do. I'm afraid to."

"Why?"

"Because it feels . . . like not just a letter."

Paxton was right to be afraid. The note itself was foul enough:

HELLO Again GOD LOVER
Cock
PRick
you know whAT I'D liKE.
ONE and A Half MILLION.
SmaLL BILLS.
you Get That Together,
ALL RigHT, BASTARD?
and HAVE IT At your
HOUSE OF Sin wAitING.
I'LL Tell you What to DO
WITH it and When.
OH YEAH. ABOUT the Little
GIFT on THE BOTTOM of the PAGE.
It couLdn't BE Anyone WE
KNOW?
LiKe your DUMPLING of a
dAUGHTER.
CouLD iT NOW?

Worse by far was the little "gift" taped to the left-hand bottom of the page. A small, wrapped piece of cellophane.
With a finger inside.

# PART III

# The Mex on Fire

# CHAPTER 1
# Medical Report

As he walked into the main bar of the Silver Spoon fifteen minutes after leaving Paxton, Escalante paused, then headed toward the near corner booth, where an expensively dressed woman was holding hands with an extraordinarily handsome dark-haired man. "This roulette system of yours, Prince; how can you be sure it really works?" the woman asked.

"You muss call me Ro-bair," the dark-haired man replied, his accent heavily French. He smiled, gently touched his lips to her fingers. "I am Prince, *oui,* but when you call me thees, eet make eet sound im-por-tann. I make the promise to you: We were the mos' un-im-por-tann royalty in the cawn-tree."

Escalante raised his hand, gestured toward the dark-haired man.

Who looked away.

Escalante repeated the gesture.

The dark-haired man ignored him, stared deeply into the eyes of the expensively dressed woman.

Escalante walked up to the booth then and said, "Sire."

"Not now, I am occupy" came the answer.

"This is very important, sire."

"Who *is* this?" the expensively dressed woman asked.

"Eeet eees my faith-fool Spanish houseboy, Garcia; sometimes hee eees too faith-fool. I weel return to the estate later, Garcia, now *be off.*"

"Your father called from France, sire—he needs to talk to you immediately—your mother isn't well."

The dark-haired man turned to the expensively dressed woman. "Shee eees often not well. I weel call late-air."

"She's dying, sire," Escalante said.

"Oh, you must go call, then," the expensively dressed woman said.

The dark-haired man hesitated, stood, "We weel talk of my sees-tem when I re-tourn, yes?"

"If I'm still here," the expensively dressed woman replied.

The dark-haired man smiled at her, scowled at Escalante, muttered "Come along, Garcia" and stormed out of the bar.

When they reached the casino area, Escalante said, "I'm sorry, I wouldn't have interrupted if it wasn't important. But it couldn't wait. I'll say it again, 'I'm sorry.' Okay?"

"Nothing is okay. You knifed me in there—why should a human being *who was supposed to be my friend* feel sorry about a little thing like that?"

Escalante sighed. There was a dramatic streak in the Frog Prince that erupted in times of upset, and all you could do was wait until it played itself out.

"Shit, it was the best goddam situation—a really rich, really dumb lady who believed everything I told her and who was about to give me a small fortune to bet using my roulette system. Ho-hum, I had that identical setup last decade." He shook his handsome head, stared up toward the eye in the sky. "*Don't* forgive him, for he knew *exactly* what he was doing." He whirled on Escalante then. "I ignored you twice—why did you butt in?"

"Because you're a brilliant doctor, Froggie."

"True and so what?—there are lots of brilliant doctors in Las Vegas." He considered that a moment. "No, that is something of an overstatement. Probably I am the only one. What's this about?"

"Something in cellophane has come into my possession and I need your expertise."

"You could have gone to the Lab Rat."

"This is more than he can handle, I suspect."

"Let me see it."

"Not here."

They headed outside then, walked along the side of the hotel. Up ahead a driveway curved into a closed entrance. Above the entrance was a cement overhang, ten feet up, six feet wide. Years ago the Silver Spoon had tried a private casino for high-rollers only. The place turned out to be a disaster—none of the big gamblers liked privacy, they wanted crowds around them, watching them. So the hotel had closed the entrance, locked it tight. Nobody much wandered past it anymore.

When they stood in the shadow of the overhang, the Frog Prince said, "Okay, what is it exactly?"

"That's what you've got to tell me," Escalante said. "I haven't opened it, just looked at it through the cellophane, and—"

The Frog Prince interrupted sharply—"Just gimme whatever it is," he said, and when Escalante handed over the cellophane package he didn't examine it, just ripped it open and dumped the contents into his hand. Then he looked at it. Then he cried out, "Shit, Nikki, this is a *finger*!"

Escalante nodded.

"You just can't give another person a finger like that. Without warning or anything."

"You all right, Froggie?"

The Frog Prince was perspiring lightly now. "How can I be all right when a man *who was supposed to be my friend* sneaks up on me like that."

"I didn't know you were squeamish, Froggie."

"It comes and it goes."

"How can you run emergency wards and be like that?"

"I throw up a lot, if you want to know." He took a deep breath, looked at Escalante. "Is this really important?"

"Really."

"Tell me what you want."

"I need every piece of information you can get from that. I want you to run every test. I want to find out sex, race, age, the works. And I need it all now."

"Christ, that could take weeks, what am I supposed to do with my rich lady inside?—"

*"—I said I needed it, Froggie!"*

The Frog Prince nodded. "Sorry. You know my best contacts are the Reno hospitals. You want me to fly up there with this?"

"I do."

"You want to tell me anything else?"

"I don't."

"Okay. I'll do everything you want." He took another deep breath, managed to bring the digit close for examination, turned it over and over in his delicate hands. "Is this a joke?" the Frog Prince asked then.

Escalante shook his head.

"I don't have to go to Reno, Nikki. I don't have to go anywhere. I can tell you everything there is to tell right here and now."

"Tell."

"Zero."

Escalante waited.

"This isn't really a finger, Nikki. I mean it is, obviously, or it was. But for your purposes, it's nothing anymore. Tell me how you got it."

"It came taped to a kidnap note."

The Frog Prince closed his eyes. "What a sick fucking world we live in."

"If I'd wanted philosophy, I'd have read my Rod McKuen; if it isn't a finger, what is it?"

"Look at your fingers."

Escalante did.

"You see the prints?"

Escalante nodded.

"That part of your skin is called the epidermis." He handed over the single digit. "Look—see? Smooth. The epidermis has been removed. And without that, it's just a hunk of meat."

Escalante studied the finger. "Would you have to be an expert to take it off? And how the hell could you get one anyway?"

"Easy. Bribe a med student, a pathologist, a guy who works in a funeral parlor, a cemetery; nothing to it. I'm not saying it would be a fun purchase, but it wouldn't be hard. And then you take it and just put it in a solvent, and in a little while, the epidermis separates naturally. It's really as easy as slipping off a glove. And when you do, you're left with this: zip. The dermis, amorphous and smooth and useless, end of lecture."

"Fug," from Escalante.

"I'll tell you the truth: Even if it hadn't been tampered with, you probably wouldn't have gotten anything—one finger is not such a much, which is why they take prints of all five." He put the finger back inside the cellophane, returned it to Escalante. "Okay with you if I go back to my rich lady now?"

Escalante nodded. They moved out from beneath the overhang into the sun, headed back toward the main entrance of the Silver Spoon. "I hear you got up to two-forty last night. Talk of the town, no shit."

Escalante said nothing.

"Christ I wish I'd been there—you should have quit, Nikki—Pinky and I, we'd have made you stop."

Escalante just gave him a look.

They walked awhile in silence then 'til the Frog Prince said, "I'm sorry. That I said that. I don't know why I did, probably I'm ticked it didn't happen to me—hell, we both know that if I'd been around I'd have begged you to go for half a million."

Escalante nodded, made a smile. "That's what friends are for," he said.

Ashley answered the bell, looked up at him. "Nicholas?"

"Madam," he said to her, as he always did in salutation.

She seemed in worse shape, more fluttery and nervous now than she had the day before, sitting by the pool, blaming herself for the sins of the world. "The Good Reverend I think is expecting me."

"Darryl isn't here—he left an hour and a half ago—he said there was a problem at The Knot—one of the children we were sheltering was becoming, he said, dangerously depressed and he thought he might be able to help."

Escalante nodded. Paxton had come to his place with the second note an hour and a half ago and they had parted then, Escalante to find the Frog Prince, Paxton to his house, he said, where he would stay.

"I'm sure he will be," Ashley said.

"Will be?"

"Able to help." Her fingers were moving unbidden; she clasped her hands in front of her, imprisoning them. "Darryl's so wonderful with children."

Escalante nodded.

There was a pause. He wondered if her lids were going to lock.

". . . Darryl's so wonderful . . ." Her voice was suddenly soft. It was almost as if she were alone and muttering to herself. Then she brightened, took his hand. "Where *have* my manners flown? Come in, come in, let's go to the living room and sit."

They went to the living room and sat. The room was slowly growing darker, it was almost four. Ashley turned on the lights, which served to emphasize the spareness of the large room, the faces of the religious paintings on the walls. "Well, now," Ashley said. She studied him. "You look weary, Nicholas."

"Hangover."

"Can I get you something?"

"No, thank you."

"Hair of the dog?"

"Really, I'm fine."

She stood. "Coffee, then? I'd like some coffee. Let me brew us a cup."

He shook his head.

"Instant coffee? Tea?"

"Let's just sit and talk."

*"You must want something."*

He looked at her, waited.

"I'm not a cripple, Nicholas. I can't drive, but I can make coffee. Perrier? Some nice Perrier with a wedge of lime."

He didn't want it but he said, "That would be lovely," because it was clear now she would never stop asking to serve.

"I'll just have the same," she said, starting out of the room, then stopping, turning back. "I don't want any Perrier and neither do you."

Escalante waited.

"I hate this so."

"Hate what, Ashley?"

"Something has entered this house. Something terrible has come to stay and no one will tell me what it is."

"I wouldn't know about that."

"Why don't I believe you?"

Escalante shrugged.

"Why are you here?"

"To see Darryl."

"About?"

"A problem."

"What kind?"

"Personal."

She looked at him with her wide blue eyes. "Damn you men and your secrets!"

The sound of the front door opening came then, followed by Paxton's voice: "I'm home." He sounded flat; there was no meaning in his words beyond the simple fact of attendance. The front door closed.

"We're in here," Ashley called.

Paxton entered, nodded to Escalante, went to Ashley, held her briefly. He looked sad or exhausted or both.

"How did it go?" Ashley asked.

He blinked.

"At The Knot. With the depressed child."

Paxton shrugged. "You never know with children. I did my best."

"That's all anyone can do," Ashley said.

"I suppose."

"Can I get you something?" Fluttering again.

"No. No, thank you, darling."

"You have the look of a man who could use some coffee."

"Really. Please. No."

"Let me do *something*."

"You do more than enough."

"I want to feel wanted," Ashley said.

"You are. You know that." He sank onto the sofa.

*"Then why are you lying to me?"*

Escalante stared at her, standing above them both, the blue eyes wide, the hands not even trying for control.

"Dear God, Ashley, when have I lied to you?"

*"Today!*—just now—I called The Knot and they said you weren't there! Hadn't been there! *Where were you?"*

Paxton shook his head. Several times. Then he said a single word: "Occupied."

She whirled to Escalante—"You see—something terrible *has* come in here"—now back to her husband—"What did I do?—tell me my sin so I can start atoning—"

And then he was up, shouting back at her—"Nothing—you did nothing—"

"—liar—"

"—stop this—"

"—liar—*liar*—"

*"—please—"* He reached out for her.

Two things happened then, all but simultaneously. She avoided his grasp, backing away, and her eyes locked, so she tripped over the coffee table, fell hard to the hardwood floor. Escalante started for her but Paxton waved him away, knelt by his wife, held her as she moaned, held her 'til the spasm lifted and her eyes were wide again, the blue there for all to see. She tried to talk but he shushed her gently, raised her up, put an arm around her, walked her away. He was gone for ten minutes. "I put her to bed," Paxton said. "It's best. She's under a strain—every time something happens to me, it happens to her. Poor sweet creature."

Escalante watched him. Paxton sank onto the couch again and looked as if he never wanted to rise. "Sorry I wasn't here to meet you. It took longer than I thought at the bank. I suppose I had a somewhat naive notion as to just what was entailed in acquiring one and a half million dollars in small bills."

"You have that much?"

"Clearly not in my checking account. But I have access to that amount and a great deal more, thanks to my parents. It should all be in place, so I'm assured, by tomorrow or the day after."

"You won't need it, Darryl, believe me. It's a nut out to cause panic, I don't think he'll ever risk breaking cover."

"Nevertheless. If he does, it's there."

"Darryl?"

"Yes."

"Explain something?"

"If I can."

"Why would you pay a ransom demand, since you don't have children?"

"Because..." Paxton began. "...Because..." he said again. Then he shook his head.

Escalante said he had nothing but time.

Paxton nodded.

Then there was silence.

Followed by Paxton enquiring did Escalante want anything? A drink perhaps? Some coffee?

Escalante shook his head.

Paxton looked in agony. "What I told you yesterday... everything I told you... about our discovery junior year, thirty years ago... the inability to conceive... about our separating on the news, Ashley to Europe, me to Africa... about our profound despair on being apart... about our marriage and our subsequent decision not to have children... all of that was true... totally totally true... every word ... except Ashley was the sterile one, not I.... I lied to you yesterday, Nicholas, but I'm telling the truth to you now...."

Escalante wasn't so sure; he made it a habit never to believe someone totally after he'd been lied to. Paxton was too upset to be making it all up. *Something* had happened to Darryl and Ashley thirty years ago and maybe it was true, what Paxton was telling now. He hoped so.

"... I'm sorry that I lied but I was trying to protect her.... Sometimes it seems I've lived my entire life trying to protect her... but it's hard to totally protect someone...."

"For 'hard' read 'impossible,'" Escalante said.

Paxton nodded. He looked dreadful now. Wasted and pale, no shred of Spencer Tracy left. "This next becomes quite... shameful. I'd much rather not continue."

"Don't."

"I have to. I have a favor to ask."

Escalante said he had nothing but time.

"I never dreamed I would be unfaithful. But then... it was shortly before you and I met, I went to Los Angeles alone for a day to do some interviews for *Owning God*. And that's when it happened."

"You slept with another woman."

Paxton shook his head. "Two."

Escalante wanted to say "Hats off" but decided against it.

"It was astonishing. They were both lovely, and even now, I like to think, they seduced me. But late afternoon I slept with the first and, of course, was stunned and filled with hate-filled recriminations and firm in the knowledge that it would never happen again and then that night it happened again. I have seen neither of them since. But I *could*—however unlikely—have impregnated one of them."

"For 'unlikely' read 'impossible.' I assume they knew you were a rich and famous fellow."

"Whatever."

"Then I guarantee you if you'd fathered a child, you'd have heard from them a long long time ago."

"Would you find out for me? Would you go there and see? That's my favor, Nicholas."

"Not such a big request."

Then Paxton said it: "Are you remotely familiar with Los Angeles?"

"Remotely familiar" was the phrase that lasted. In the rest of the time he spent with Paxton, gathering data. In the time he spent with Pinky, considering possible contingencies. During the phone call he had with Kinnick, saying he hadn't forgotten him, just hadn't decided one way or the other. During the rush to the airport, to catch the late flight.

Was he "remotely familiar"? He'd been born there. He had lived almost the first sixteen years of his life in Los Angeles. In the arguably largest estate on Stone Canyon Road in the heart of Bel-Air. He had killed his good father there. No. That was overdramatizing. He hadn't killed him, just caused him to die.

But that counted. . . .

# CHAPTER 2

# Stranger in a Foreign Land

Whenever he awoke in Los Angeles, in his mind there was always Miranda.

Trying to travel someplace was pointless—he could not banish her, she was simply there, behind his eyes, lush and urging, eighteen, dark skin, dark eyes, dark hair. It was night, and they were standing across the enormous swimming pool from one another. He was not much more than a kid, had been infatuated with her from the beginning. The night was starless. The only light came from below the waterline of the pool.

The estate was deserted. No cars moved on Stone Canyon Road. He was alone on the place, or thought he had been alone. She was away at college. Or had been. Now she was suddenly there. So *they* were alone on the place. She turned her back to him, moved her hands. The top part of the suit was loose, then off. She stepped out of the bottom. When she turned back to him, she did it very slowly. The force of her pivot on him was sudden and strong. He just stared at her, at her splendid body and dark skin, dark except where the suit had been; that flesh was pale.

Now she smiled at him. "... take off yours ..."

"... shouldn't ..."

She laughed.

He stood there.

"... not interested ... ?"

He shook his head.

She pointed to his bathing trunks. "... then what's that ... ?"

He put his hands over the front of his suit.

"... do I have to take it off for you ...?"

He knew he should run.

"... little baby, has to have everything done for him ..."

It was very important that he leave her, right away, he knew that, because what if they were caught, what then?

Singsong now: "...baby, baby, soak your head in gravy..." And then slowly she began to move around the pool toward him. "... bay-bee ... bay-bee ..."

He could do nothing but watch as she drew nearer.

When she was close, she stopped, lightly kissed his lips, ran her fingers down his body. Then she knelt slowly in front of him, reached out, pulled his bathing suit down and off as his penis sprang free.

It was precisely ten in the morning when he pulled up in front of Arnold Wylie's house in the flats of Beverly Hills, a one-story standard brand California/Mexican/ugly set between Sunset and Little Santa Monica.

He reached for the notebook and ball-point beside him on the seat. Then he got out of the car, hurried toward the front door. It was raining, not hard, not hard yet at least, and he was wearing his best and only suit, the blue, with a white shirt and dark tie and cordovans. It was his most respectable costume; at least that was the theory.

He rang, waited, but not long. The woman who answered was small, five two perhaps, expensively dressed, green-eyed, thirty. "Mrs. Wylie?" he asked.

She was. "You're the guy who called, have I got it?"

He nodded in an exaggerated manner, talked both more quickly and with a higher tone than usual—he had always been able to do a decent enough "prissy" and he decided to go along with it now. "Oh, yes, I'm the very one. And I thank you ever so much for seeing me, it's so thoughtful of you and all, considering the short notice, I mean, and I swear to you, on my oath, I won't take long."

She studied him a moment before saying, "Don't have long." Then she gestured for him to follow her inside. It was on the twenty-step journey to the bookless library that he realized she was perfectly beautiful. The key word being "perfectly." He had seen any number of beautiful women over the years, but usually you sensed it the instant they entered. Mrs. Arnold Wylie wasn't like that; it took a while for her to register. Perhaps because she was small. More than likely, though, it was the flawlessness. Escalante had seen John Derek walking along the street once, and it wasn't for a good moment that he realized the woman walking with him was his wife. She wasn't dressed to be recognized, true, but she was perfect too. And probably could walk unnoticed wherever and whenever she wanted.

They sat and she looked at her watch. "I shoulda put this off, I can't be late for my Aspiring class and with the weather like this, you can't figure the traffic."

Ordinarily he would have let that pass, but part of Los Angeles still fascinated him, the nut groups as much as any single thing. There were way over two thousand of them that had been officially catalogued—"self-improvement" organizations, "end of the world" societies, on and on. No one could even guess at how many more thousand unofficial groups existed. L.A. was really a foreign country, no more representative of America than Barbuda or Qatar or Vanuatu.

"I'm interested in Aspiring myself," he said. "I almost took a Manifesting seminar myself last year, it's the same thing, isn't it?"

"The same? *The same?*" Suddenly the green eyes were bright. "Manifesting, and this is strictly fact, no insult intended, is for weirdos, the kind of people who have it in their heads that San Francisco is chic. Aspiring is strictly class."

"Very Los Angeles, you mean, have I got it?"

She nodded. "One guy who graduated last month, he

came back and gave our class a talk—he aspired to a condo in Hawaii and guess what?—a cousin of his kicked suddenly and left him enough bread to buy one."

"Wishing will make it so, I guess. At least sometimes."

"Aspiring isn't wishing—anyone can wish—you have to have mental discipline before you can Aspire."

She tossed her head slightly when she said "mental discipline" and it told him a couple of things: She thought of herself as an actress, and she had recently heard the phrase someplace, liked it, had newly added it to her vocabulary.

"Why do you look so familiar, have I seen you on the television, I'll bet I have," he said, going on the first notion.

She touched her light brown hair. "I did a Prell commercial once."

"Maybe that was it." He smiled. She was looking at her watch frequently now but he doubted she was in as much of a hurry as she was jittery, concerned, apprehensive, pick one. He opened his notebook, readied the ball-point pen. "I'm here, as I think I told you on the phone, because of my interest in Darryl Paxton; in point of fact, I'm writing what I hope will be the definitive biography of the man"—he made a little chuckle then—"of course, it would be hard for it *not* to be the definitive biography because it will be the first—but what I mean is that I hope, when I'm done, it stands the test of time."

"Go on."

"Well, personally, Mrs. Wylie, when I set out to write a book, particularly a biography such as this one, I believe that the crucial element toward making such an endeavor a success is in research—I'm a devoted believer in exhaustive research and that, of course, is the reason we are together this dreary morning."

She waited.

"You see, although, as I've said, this is going to be, if God is on my side, definitive, it is not, I must be honest, what you might call, 'authorized'—but I have it on what I consider very good authority that when the Reverend Paxton visited Los Angeles approximately six years ago, you two came in contact and what I want, at least to begin with, are any impressions of the man that you might recall which could be helpful to me and, by extension, my readers about what he was like then."

"That's everything you're after, have I got it?"

Escalante nodded.

She began to laugh then. "Aw, Christ, am I sorry," she said after a while. "You just gotta forgive me."

"Of course, Mrs. Wylie, for what?"

"This is all a mistake. On the phone, I didn't hear you good—you said Paxton but what I heard was . . . see, the cofounder of my Los Angeles Aspiring chapter is named Frank *Gax*ton and I thought you wanted, I don't know, maybe a quote from me about how much I like the Aspiring course."

"You don't know Darryl Paxton, then?"

"Never met the man."

Escalante stood quickly. "Don't worry, I've had many greater confusions in my research travels. And I'm staying at the Wilshire so it's what, a five-minute drive? I'm sorry I bothered you at all." They started toward the front door then. "Lovely home, may I say—can I ask you a question?"

"Go."

"With all you have, why are you Aspiring? You own so much."

"I want a bigger pool—I'm into lap swimming—and a Maserati to shop in. I got a long list, believe me." She opened the front door.

"Good-bye," Escalante said, and this time *he* started laughing.

"Is that so funny, wanting things?"

"Excuse me, Mrs. Wylie, it wasn't that at all, it's just I realized what the confusion was—you see, I made a mistake, it's not you I should have seen, it's *Mister* Wylie. Yes, I'm sure that is it." He opened his notebook, wrote quickly for a moment. "I'll give him a hoot on the horn from the Wilshire as soon as I'm done with my other appointment, probably around noon, catch him before lunch." The rain was harder now. He stepped out into it, started for the car, was not surprised to hear her call after him.

"Hey?"

Escalante turned.

"He's a very busy man, Arnie."

"I'm sure he is."

"He's not into religion."

"So few of us are these days."

"I don't think he knows any Paxton."

"Of course he doesn't," Nick Escalante said.

If the Wylie house would go for maybe a million, and it would, the Dutton Granger estate would take at least ten times that amount if ever it went up for sale. An enormous Mediterranean-style two-story villa, it was set back, invisible from Mulholland Drive, in one of the more celebrated parts of the city; Brando supposedly lived nearby, Nicholson too. The reason for the expense was more than the privacy—there was no better view of the city anywhere.

At least, when it wasn't raining. Escalante, as he waited at the front door, couldn't see shit, not in this December storm. Thunder had begun in the fifteen minutes it had taken him to drive from the flats, and it showed no signs of stopping.

The butler or chauffeur or houseman or whatever the hell his uniform represented indicated for Escalante to remain in the glassed-in patio. "I'll see that Mrs. Granger is alerted," he said. The accent was so heavily British it made you want to break something.

Escalante smiled, at some cost. Then he was alone, staring at the grey outside the window, listening to the rain as it grew heavier, splattering against the glass of the patio, approximating hail. The ceiling of the patio was also glass and he contented himself with staring up at it, watching the drops flatten. When he was aware that he was no longer alone, he turned.

The woman walking in was a California nightmare. Clad in tennis whites, her skin was overly tanned, unpleasantly leatherlike. She was in her early forties, with a silly, streaked-blond hairdo that in theory was gaminlike, in practice added years. There was no telling how much surgery she had undergone. Certainly the bags had been removed from beneath her eyes. Clearly she had had at least two nose jobs, one for straightening, another inside, to replace the cartilage between her nostrils that cocaine had eaten away. The number of tummy tucks or ass lifts was unknowable. Worse than anything else was her body. Or the remains of her body. Any high school girl with anorexia would have been jealous. The woman stood five six, could not have weighed ninety pounds. Whatever the L.A. dream was once, she was it gone haywire.

There was a very long silence before Escalante was able to speak. Finally, with great effort, he said it: "Hello, Miranda."

She looked at him blankly.

He held very tightly to his notebook, waited for recognition.

She looked at him blankly.

"It's Nick Escalante, Miranda."

A flicker crossed somewhere behind her eyes. She moved up close to him, staring so hard.

He stood still, wondering what, at this early hour, she was on.

"Oh, God, Nick, you've changed so."

"I know."

"You look so old."

"Not you. You look the same as then."

"Well, I work out a lot."

"That explains it."

She nodded. "I have a private strength coach comes here three times a week, and I watch every single thing I put in my mouth—you can't be too careful with your body, not with the preservatives they stick in stuff nowadays."

He shifted his weight from one foot to the other. She was still staring at him. He had no idea what she was seeing.

"Nick Escalante," Miranda said then.

"That's right."

She smiled. "You wouldn't be here if it weren't for me."

He nodded. "You're the one I came to see, right again."

"No-no—that's not it—what I meant was, you never would have met Paxton if it hadn't been for me."

"I don't know about that."

She took his hand, walked him to the window. "Well, I do. That day *I* met Paxton, he told me he was getting all kinds of wild, dangerous stuff in the mail and he was from Vegas and there was an article about you. Someone I knew from back then sent it to me with a note that said something like 'Is this the same one who used to live over your garage on Stone Canyon?' and when I read about you, I knew it was. So I told Paxton, if he ever needed help with the crazies out there, to go see Nick Escalante and he'd fix everything."

Escalante nodded, thinking back to his interview with Chief of Detectives Galloway the day he'd first met the Paxtons, and Galloway had said he'd given Paxton several names but Escalante was the one he'd chosen. "He's a minister, maybe he likes ethnics," Galloway had said. Something like that. And all the time the reason was Miranda. "Thank you for the endorsement."

"I had faith—you were such a good kid, well brought up and all, and you were strong even then. You were in some kind of shape. All my girl friends used to go on about you."

He said nothing.

She began to lose it then. "You were in good shape then, I'm in good shape now."

"That's right."

". . . I work out a lot is why. . . ."

He nodded.

". . . I have . . . a man comes to see me three times . . . a coach, he keeps me . . . what did we used to say, 'in the pink'?"

"That's what we used to say."

Now her body was losing it, too, and there were tears as she said, "Aw, Nick, it's been such shit," and then she was in his arms, kissing his mouth, her bone arms clutching his body and at first he held back but after a moment he couldn't, it would be an act beyond cruelty, so he held her, returned her pressure, gave her his tongue to suckle as her body slapped hard against his. And then she began to go slack, and he had to support her or let her fall, and once his arms were cradling her, she relaxed even more so that he had to lift her entirely, which he did, no problem, she was weightless and his arms were the source of his power. She gestured toward the door and when he was outside, there was a wide staircase and, feeling like Gable with Leigh in his arms, he began to walk up and then he met the uniformed butler or whatever with the accent on the stairs and the butler averted his eyes and Escalante almost stopped, but how could he explain, so feeling like the fool of all the world, aware that the uniformed man was watching him all the way to the top, he continued with the blond bony lady weeping in his arms. The master bedroom was gigantic, all glass, and the view, when there was a view, probably was worth it, but now there was terrible rain sound, dreadful thunder, as they began to undress, and Escalante never knew how he rated with women, he knew he enjoyed it most when he cared most, when he could be gentle, but did he linger in the memories of ladies he'd been with was something he never was sure of.

The Frog Prince was the reigning expert on the subject, and sometimes would hold forth, not so much on technique, but on categories. And the best kind of lovemaking was what he called "silver sex," when two people were very in love with each other, that was wonderful except it never happened, and "spite sex" was good, if you were honest enough to admit it, and hard was "Old Glory sex," when you had to, for reasons of business, not pleasure. Hardest of all, though, the killer, was "should-have-been sex," when two pasts too late rekindled. Escalante was into that now, he knew, a should-have-been time, and he closed his eyes, blotting out the leather skeleton beneath him, thinking only of the glory across the swimming pool with her bathing suit slowly coming down, her breasts white for not the world but just for him to see, and he watched her slowly walk around toward him, kneel, take off his own suit, reveal him hard and naked and now, as he mounted, he prayed to be able to retain the past, that his cock, working in the present, would not choose this sad moment to betray him.

It didn't.

"Do you want anything?" Miranda asked. They were lying together on the bed, listening to the pounding of the rain.

He shook his head.

"Uppers or downers, grass?"

"No."

"Coke, then?"

Escalante looked at her and thought of Ashley, fluttering the afternoon before, offering him coffee, tea, Perrier. "I'm not much into foreign substances before lunch."

"You must want something."

"I do. Tell me about you and Darryl Paxton."

"Tell you what?"

"The works."

"Are you aware of anything?"

"Yes, that you're neither of you virgins, if that makes it any easier."

"It does and it doesn't." She sat up then, cross-legged, ran her hands along his body. "How did you get the scars?" she said, pointing to his legs.

"Bomb."

"You didn't have them when we knew each other; I remember your body too well."

"You and Paxton, Miranda."

"Ah, yes, Sadie Thompson and the Reverend Davidson."

"Quit the dodging."

"I seduced him, sure. He was quite unaware I think of just how attractive he was. Very shy, *very* appealing." She paused. "I'm trying to remember precisely when this was."

"Six years ago."

"Yes, of course, silly me, I'd been married less than a month, I shouldn't have forgotten." She lay down again, moving close to him. When the next thunderclap died, she started talking. "He was in town I think for a night, doing publicity. *Owning God,* wasn't it?"

"It was."

"He was very feted. Interviews, a luncheon, someone else gave a dinner, all that kind of thing. Very sought after, a different kind of star. Like Sandy Koufax was a decade before. I was invited to the luncheon and I didn't look like this then, my hair was darker, I was fat, at least one-twenty. But some men liked me and Paxton I could tell was one of them, though he hadn't the least notion of how to go about accomplishing his aims. So I offered, after the lunch, to drive him to his hotel and on the way I asked had he ever seen the view from the top of Mulholland and he said he hadn't so we came here, to this house, then to this room. It wasn't hard to get him into bed." She moved even closer to Escalante then, resting her head against his cheek.

He lay very still, aware of the flutter of her eyelids, of the moisture from her tears.

"It was . . . not a good time for me, you see. My first husband had been a failure, my next a fag, and when

Dutton, so rich and so beautiful—our fathers were competitors in the real estate business, the joke was that ours wasn't a marriage, it was a merger—at any rate, dear glorious Dutton, silly me was a bit jarred to discover, was both a fag *and* a failure, so when the Reverend appeared, although briefly, in my life, I wanted him, so very badly—I was very rocky and I needed his goodness inside me. And that, thank the Lord, is the end of the saga."

"I don't think so, Miranda. If it was, you wouldn't be crying."

When she got control of herself again she ran her finger down his chest. "Such a clever boy." Then she listened to the thunder echoing through the canyon below.

Escalante waited. It was strange, staring out, because there was nothing but grey beyond the window, they might have been in some spaceship in a world without sun.

"Chapter two, the pregnancy, that's the juicy part, after all. Dutton was capable of having sex with a woman, he could have been the father, except he wasn't, he never knew I was pregnant because he ran off to Hawaii with a simply stunning young shoe salesman he met at Gucci's. I haven't spoken to him in years, but we'll never divorce, he saves me from remarrying again. He's got an estate, I'm told, in one of the out islands and what irritates me, I suppose, is he's still with that goddam little twerp from the wop store. I didn't show for a while and I thought I could gut it through here but it turned out I lacked gall, so off I went to the most glorious stately home outside London that I rented until delivery. I'd never had a child before and many people, most people, will tell you of the pain, and of course it's true. But it wasn't true for me. Because through all the hurt I knew I had my very own companion coming and she would never run away, I would never again be alone."

"You had a girl then."

"I like to think so. Because—when your legs were damaged,

I'll bet it hurt—well, I hurt, too, when they told me, the good British doctors, that the child was so hopelessly retarded it would be best if I knew nothing, never saw it or touched it, 'Just put it out of your mind.' I love male doctors. No one's invented a 'just put it out of your mind' pill yet. Anyway, somewhere in England is the flesh of my flesh, and my accountant sends funds monthly, sufficient for its needs. And that *is* the end of the saga."

He thought it best to hold her for a while.

They listened to the rain until she asked, "Do you remember the last time we were together, the Stone Canyon place, by the pool?"

"No."

"You must have blocked it—I do that sometimes, when there's stuff I don't want to think about."

"I must have done that, then."

"It was the closest we ever got to sleeping together—we were buff naked and I was kneeling in front of you touching you when my goddam father found us—I'll never forget his screaming. I thought he was going crazy. I never saw him angry like that—it didn't matter to him how long your folks had worked for us—all my life I think."

"I had a crush on you. They knew it. I remember promising them never to go near you. I guess they were scared something would happen."

"I was so mad at my father for firing them. I didn't know 'til later he told everyone your folks had been stealing from us. When I found out, it was all I could do not to really let him have it. But when you're an only child and your old man's worth *mucho dinero,* I guess it does things for your discipline."

"The rich are different from you and me, they have more discipline." He sat up, put his feet on the floor.

"Where did you go after we got rid of you?"

"Different places."

"With your folks?"

"Well, he died." Escalante stood.

She stared at him. "Downstairs? The minute I walked in, I knew it was you, you haven't changed, I lied because I couldn't stand you seeing me not at my best."

"You're a great-looking woman and that's the truth."

"I guess. But I just know I wouldn't be if I didn't keep after myself."

"That's a very positive way to think."

"Now that you know how to get here, you'll come back."

"Try and stop me."

"Are you lying?"

"I never lie."

Now she came off the bed and her arms went around him, and they walked naked together to the window. "The view, it'll just knock you sideways."

"Something to look forward to."

"We could have been so happy, Nick."

"I'm happy now," Nick Escalante said.

Silently he audited the rain. . . .

It was noon when, soaked and shaken, he entered the lobby of the Beverly Wilshire, asked for his messages. There were three, all in the last hour and a half. "Call me, Mrs. Arnold Wylie," then "Please call, Rainbeaux Wylie" and finally, "Waiting for you, Rainbeaux." He noted the increasing familiarity, realized that at least in this case absence did make the heart grow fonder, was on his way to his room to change and call when Fred Astaire came up to him, gave him a hug.

It wasn't Astaire, of course; still, it was not possible to see The Glider without thoughts of the greatest dancer flashing by. The Glider must have been sixty now and, as always, perfectly dressed, complete to the powder-blue silk shirt, the casually tied ascot. More than attire forced Astaire to mind—no one Escalante had ever met moved with the assurance, the quick grace of The Glider, which, Escalante guessed, decades past, was where his name had come from.

The Glider was a hugger and Escalante stood in the lobby while the smaller, thin man held him. "Nikki, Nikki, Nikki, what a glorious surprise, come on, now, show some affection," and Escalante sighed, returned the embrace, because he knew The Glider would never let him go until he did.

They broke, examined each other. There was no question, the Mex felt, that this chance meeting had to be a positive—no one cheered him like The Glider did, bad jokes and all. They had worked together more than a little, The Glider owed him more than a lot.

The Glider said "Coffee," not as a question, and they headed down the hall past the barbershop. Escalante flicked a glance at The Glider's hands, because The Glider always said to do that, because that way you'd know how business was—once his hands went, well, forget about everything. Whatever Escalante was from twenty feet in, The Glider was for up to twenty yards—he was the monarch of handguns, and there were no pretenders for his throne. Shrink the bull's-eye all you wanted, The Glider could blow it away.

He held up his hands now. "Steady as rocks," he said.

"I'm not surprised," Escalante said, wondering when The Glider caught his glance. "What does surprise me is the dirt under your fingernails."

"Dirt? Dirt?—*where?*" The Glider said, stopping dead, examining his hands. He had a fetish about cleanliness, particularly when it came to his fingers. Now he broke out laughing. "Oh, Nikki, Nikki, Nikki, still teasing at your age, for shame." They entered the coffee shop, took the booth nearest the door, and before they were even settled, The Glider said "Gorilla story. A gorilla walks into Muldoon's Bar—perhaps you know Muldoon's, over in Santa Monica."

"Never heard of it," Escalante said, smiling and thinking, At these prices, you never will.

"This beast orders a martini on the rocks and the bartender doesn't quite know what to do, so he goes to Muldoon in the back and explains and Muldoon thinks that he doesn't want his bar becoming a hangout for gorillas but on the other hand, he doesn't want the animal wrecking his joint so he says, 'Give him the drink but charge him twenty dollars,' so the bartender makes the martini and the gorilla pays the twenty and while he's sipping it, quite daintily I might add, the bartender sidles over and says, 'You know, we don't get many gorillas in here,' and the gorilla replies, 'At these prices, you never will.'" He waited for Escalante's laugh, joined it. "Truly a joyous tale, is it not so?"

"Truly."

The Glider made an imaginary toast, said "Two coffees" to the waitress as she approached. She nodded, turned and The Glider said, "Golf story. Mulcahy and Ryan are playing golf and Ryan slices a shot into the woods—very swampy course they're attacking, I might add—and Ryan says, 'That's my favorite golf ball, I'm not about to lose it,' so into the woods he plunges, where, before he can find his shot, he disturbs a rattlesnake who is so put out he bites Ryan on the end of his dong. Ryan staggers back to Mulcahy, explains what happened, collapses on the grass and mutters 'Call the doctor,' so Mulcahy races to the nearest phone and explains everything to the medico, who says, 'Just take it easy, all you have to do is make two little crosses by the bite and then just use your mouth and suck out all the poison,' and Mulcahy says, 'Let me see if I've got this, I just make two little crosses by the wound and put my mouth there and suck out the poison,' and the doctor answers 'Perfect' and Mulcahy rushes back out on the course to Ryan who asks, 'What did the doctor say?' and Mulcahy answers, 'He says you're gonna die.'"

The Glider roared at that and Escalante did, too, and it was during these moments, just before their coffee came, that he suddenly knew that their meeting was not an accident, not even close.

"Thank you, beloved," The Glider said to the waitress, and before she had turned he was saying, "Shaggy-dog story."

Escalante bent down, lifted his cup halfway, blew on the too-hot liquid, wondering what it all was, because The Glider had killed God only knew how many, but he had never been deceitful, and surely he was being that now.

"Workman opens his lunch pail, great big fellow, takes out his food, stares at it and yells, 'Peanut butter sandwiches, I hate peanut butter sandwiches,' and he throws it into the wastebasket. Next day, he opens his lunch pail and says, 'Peanut butter sandwiches, I *hate* peanut butter sandwiches!' and this time he picks it up and slams it against the wall. Third day he opens his pail and screams, *'Peanut butter sandwiches, I hate peanut butter sandwiches,'* and another workman, little elf of a fellow, says, 'Hey, mister, why don't you tell your wife what you like and what you don't,' and the big guy turns on him and roars, 'YOU LEAVE MY WIFE OUT OF THIS, I MAKE MY OWN PEANUT BUTTER SANDWICHES.'" He threw back his head and let his laughter fly.

Escalante sipped his coffee.

The Glider quieted. "Oh, you've heard that one?"

"I've heard them all."

"You've just stopped being polite, is that it?"

Escalante shrugged.

"Don't be surly with me, darlin'."

"No one can be. Not for very long."

"I do have my Irish charm, don't I?"

"No one has more."

Now they both sipped coffee. Outside, the thunder had moved on, leaving the rain to carry on alone. "Aw, Nikki, Nikki, Nikki, you're a shrewd one, not one for small talk, a hard man, a very hard man." The Glider sighed. "Oh, how I wish today were yesterday."

"Stop dancing."

"How can I put this?—although 'tis always 'glorious'

seeing you, 'twas hardly, as I put it, a 'surprise.' I called Pinky, he said you were staying here."

"I figured that."

Now there was a very long pause, and suddenly the charm was gone, the leprechaun on quick vacation, and there was age in the unsmiling eyes. "The wife's not well," The Glider said, the subtext apparent.

"Terminal?"

"So the medicos would have us believe."

"Well, I'm sorry; she was very kind to me."

"To everybody."

Escalante waited.

"There's a clinic in Mexico I just heard of. I want to take her there—radical, but sometimes you have to take chances."

Escalante waited.

"It's not, alas, inexpensive; you'd think, Mexico and all, with what's happened to the peso and all, it would be cheap, but the costs are ferocious."

Nothing from Escalante.

The Glider looked across the table. "You're not going to help me out at all, are you?"

Escalante waited.

The Glider reached across the table, patted Escalante's hand. "I've been offered seventy-five thousand for you, Nikki; a fine old Italian family in Lexington, the DeMarcos, I've done business with them in the past, though never on this financial level. You should feel very proud, Nikki—when Joey Gallo went, the price was only fifty. Doesn't that give you a sense of accomplishment?"

"And you said yes?"

The Glider raised his hand for the waitress, flashed her a smile, which brought her quickly. "If you could just freshen this, I'd be forever in your servitude," he said, and he waited while she poured, smiled again when she was finished, muttered his thanks. "I haven't given them an answer. As of this moment. I couldn't, not 'til I talked to you."

Escalante stared at the professional Irishman across the table. "Jesus Christ, are you here because you want *me* to give *you* permission to kill *me*?"

"You have grasped the concept perfectly."

"How are your kids?" Escalante asked.

"Alive. Alive and well. All thanks to you. Don't think this is an easy day for me; I'm suffering. Truly. If the money weren't so paramount, I would have slammed the phone down, I promise you."

"What if I say no?"

"Oh, Nikki, Nikki, Nikki, you won't and you can't—you don't want my wife on your conscience; and you're angry at me as we sit here; and you don't want to find out what I'd do if you did say no. And most of all, of course, you're intrigued." Now he leaned close, began to whisper. "You and I, Nikki—and only the cream shall rise. Think of it—in future decades people will be talking of us still—legends—we're like Ali and Frazier, Nikki, we're both great alone, but together, as opponents, we can have eternity."

Escalante reached idly for the saltshaker, unscrewed the metal cap, ran his finger over the edge. "Why don't I kill you now?" he asked.

"Because you're you—and you care for me—because you won't and you can't—because deep down, you don't think I'll come kill you, I owe you too much."

Escalante sat back and closed his eyes for a moment, wondering was it just two days before when he had visited the gorge and watched the sunset on Annapurna? And then Bible-Face was talking about the "untrustworthy town"? And Osgood Percy had charged in, all triumphant, because true love had come calling. And Holly had gone away while Miranda, horribly, reentered, and all before the kidnap notes and their madness and his own madness, when he held two-forty in his hands and had to piss it all away. Escalante, eyes still closed, shook his head. He felt, for the first time, not beaten, not exhausted, just ready to pack it in permanently. "Where and when?" he asked quietly.

"Oh, I think Vegas would be the logical place. I have to return to Tahoe, gather what I need, I should reach Vegas by sundown tonight easily. Whenever you get there, I'll be waiting. But I make you this promise because of what we are to each other: I'll let you know before I act. I'll give you every chance to defend yourself. Or if you like, to run."

"It would seem to me—if I was an old fart and desperate—that I'd say just what you said: 'I'll let you know first'—and then I wouldn't do it. Catch me off guard."

The Glider smiled. "Indeed, it may come to that." He studied the larger man. "But I doubt it. I heard about what happened to you at the blackjack table. Your past is catching up with you, I fear."

"Is that psychological warfare?"

"Oh, Nikki, Nikki, beloved Nikki, I don't need to resort to trickery—we both know you have no chance at all of surviving against me."

"Why is that?"

"It's in your face, darlin'—you don't care—I want to live more than you do—and so I will—and so I will—"

Escalante sipped his coffee. Nothing much to say. He knew a truth when he heard one. . . .

"That was all hooey, about you being a writer, have I got it?" Mrs. Wylie asked. They were back in her bookless library. Everything was much the same, only now the rain had departed, the thunder, at least momentarily, replacing it with considerable vengeance.

"We both specialize in hooey, Mrs. Wylie."

"Rainbeaux. That's 'b-e-a-u-x,' not 'b-o-w.'"

"Strictly class," Escalante said. He sat on the sofa, watched as she brought her legs up under her body in the easy chair.

"That's not my show-business name, I was born with it—my mother was an extra, and she figured I'd have the talent."

Escalante nodded. At their first meeting, she had been ladylike, dressed for Aspiring. Now she was ready for action. She wore a short beige skirt, a white silk blouse without a bra; the blouse was unbuttoned precisely one button more than it should have been. Her sexuality was luggage she was lumbered with and now the suitcase was unlocked. "Was it your talent that attracted Darryl Paxton? You knew him, have I got it?"

"I admit I didn't exactly tell the whole truth before."

"You didn't tell *any* of the truth before."

She thought about that. "I guess, if you want to get technical."

"That's what I want to get."

She flicked a thumbnail against her upper front teeth.

Probably that meant she was thinking, Escalante decided.

"Okay, the reason I lied before—all that 'Gaxton' instead of 'Paxton' bull—was, I wanted to see you to see how much you knew and when you came on about the book I figured I was safe, you didn't know anything, and then when you snuck in that remark about seeing my husband, I knew I was wrong, you'd been stringing me, probably you knew everything and I better head you off at the pass. Did you call him?"

"I would have if you hadn't called me."

"I figured." She began doing the tooth-fingernail business again.

"Six years ago was when you met Paxton."

"You got it."

Escalante waited for her to start.

Tick/tick/tick went the nail. "Sometimes you hate to go back in time, it's such shit in there."

"I see you've read your Schopenhauer," Escalante said.

She looked at him a moment.

"He teaches rolfing at U.C.L.A."

"Oh. Right, right."

Tick/tick/tick. Then: "It was all on account of Cheryl Ladd."

"It was?"

Rainbeaux got up, went to the windows, listened to the thunder recede. "See, I almost got the part on *Charlie's*

*Angels* when Farrah left—my agent swore it was down to me and Ladd—and then I heard, my agent did, that maybe they were gonna need a new girl, that maybe Ladd would blow—I really wanted that part, but, you know, getting kicked in the teeth and losing the first time, well, my confidence was down, I was damn near surrounded by negative vibes. And Arnie and me got invited to a party for Paxton one night he was in town doing hype and I figured, the minute I met him, he could be my salvation, I mean, here he was, a good man, a minister, for Chrissakes, what better than a minister to chase the bad vibes away, and . . ." She turned, looked at Escalante. "Besides, I'd never fucked one."

"Don't look at me, neither have I."

She moved across the room again, sat close beside him on the couch. "He was staying at the Beverly Hills. I set it up with my mother, she called in, said she was sick, I told Arnie I'd go be with her, she knew to cover if he tumbled, but he never did. I went to Paxton's hotel, got him on the house phone, said I knew it was late but I was kind of in torment and would he help and, well, once I got into his room the rest was, I don't mean to be conceited, but men, they don't mind being around me a whole lot. I stayed with him a little after, and we prayed some, for my well-being and all, but I didn't get on goddam *Charlie's Angels* anyway." She moved closer to him on the couch, studying his face. "You look like that tennis player—" she said then—tick/tick/tick—

"I know," Escalante answered.

"Nastase, that's the guy."

"Everybody tells me the same thing." For a moment he wondered if he should let her make her move, so, like Paxton, he could be seduced twice in the same day. But there was really no hard decision to make—once had been more than plenty. Never was more than plenty if you didn't care. "Why are you so frightened of your husband in all this?"

"I'm not frightened—I'd just rather leave it where Jesus flung it—Arnie can get his dander up and he did the Paxton night—"

"—he didn't buy the story with your mother."

"No—but on my way out of the hotel I ran into a guy he'd lent money to to start a business and a week later the guy ran into Arnie and when I got pregnant, Arnie thought Paxton was maybe the father and beat up on me a little."

Escalante stared at her. "A girl, have I got it?"

Rainbeaux nodded. "Sunshine—I named her myself—she's got the talent, too, I can tell."

"Where is she?"

"One block over, playing with a friend, I don't want you seeing her, she might tell Arnie. She's not the kind of kid forgets anything, my looks and Arnie's brains, she's already almost got a Kellogg's commercial."

"*Is* Paxton the father?"

"Possible, but I don't much think so. Could have been Arnie. But there was a record producer I was kind of seeing a lot of too—a whole lot of, and him Arnie never tumbled to—I'm an even greater singer than actress, I can give cards and spades to Linda Ronstadt but I can't get the break." She shook her head. "That producer? He drowned four years ago in a storm at Malibu. Boy, do I have shit luck." Her eyes flicked toward Escalante now. "You don't have any friends in the business, do you?"

"Sorry." He stood.

She stood too, buttoned the button on her blouse, walked him to the front door. "The way I look at things, we don't ever have to talk again."

"You got it."

"And you won't nose around, asking Arnie anything."

"My right hand to God," Nick Escalante said.

* * *

"My name," Nick Escalante said to Arnold Wylie, "is Franky Gambino." He reached out his hand, let Wylie win the shaking battle. "I 'preciate you seeing me, a man like you. This, here, is my card." He put it on the desk.

Arnold Wylie smiled, said, "Have a chair, Mr. Gambino." He glanced across his office, on a high floor in one of the buildings at Century City. Wylie's office was unusual—very plush but very small—there was just a receptionist's area and his room.

Wylie's lone employee stood in the doorway. Filled it, really. Escalante glanced back at her. She was a world away from Rainbeaux. Tall, nearing six feet, big-shouldered, big breasts, with a hawk nose, fierce eyes. Escalante turned away, thinking he never wanted her mad at him. "That will be all, Miss Rucker," Arnold Wylie said.

"Yessir, Mr. Wylie," Miss Rucker said, with a voice that was all wrong. It was very soft, breathy, almost little-girlish, a Jackie Onassis sound.

When they were alone, Arnold Wylie picked up the card Escalante had given him. "'Roth Associates.' I don't know your firm."

"We're as big as any in Vegas. Twenty-five lawyers and growing every year. I know that's no big deal to an L.A. guy, but twenty-five and growing is not to be sneezed at where I come from."

"Am I to take it you're a lawyer, Mr. Gambino?"

"No, no, sir, I'm more in the business end of the practice, like that."

Arnold Wylie said nothing for a while. He sat, clocking Escalante, never taking his eyes away. "Husky" was the word for Wylie. Five seven, fifty-five, he could have taken over the lead in *Lou Grant* if Ed Asner had ever gotten sick. He was dressed conservatively for the city, suit with vest, button-down shirt, striped tie. "Are you for real?" he said finally.

"Pardon, Mr. Wylie?"

"I've done a lot of business in Vegas, I go there often, and I repeat, I never heard of you guys. You call up out of the blue and you say you want to talk business with me, business worth maybe millions to us both. Well, people just don't do that. That's why I said I'd see you. Curiosity." He looked at his watch. "It's two-forty. You've got ten minutes."

"Well, that's kind of putting me under the gun, 'specially when you consider what might be at stake here, in terms of financially speaking."

"Why don't you very quickly tell me just what might be 'at stake' here?"

Escalante pulled at his collar. "Well, like I said, we're a firm on the come—"

"—I know, twenty-five and growing."

"Right. And one of the reasons for our success is, we like to think aggressively. A lot of our clients have a lot of money and we sometimes come up with ways to make them more. The reason I'm here to see you is, well, I don't have to flatter you, you know who you are, you're one of the top adventure capitalists in town."

"*Ven*ture capitalist, Mr. Gambino."

"Right, absolutely."

"I think perhaps I better speak to your Mr. Roth."

"There's no need to bother him none!—it's simple—you fork over dough for new businesses. A guy has an idea, if you like it, you back him and if he hits, you got stock rights. Sometimes it's a two-seventy–to–one return. Well, we can put together a deal for you—some of our clients want to give *you* their money to invest for them—they'll ride on your rep, Mr. Wylie."

"What business are your clients in?"

"Hotel."

"They're owners, executives?"

Escalante fidgeted a moment. "More into the garbage end of it—collection from hotels. And the laundry part, napkins, tablecloths, et cetera."

Wylie smiled, pushed the intercom, said, "Miss Rucker, get me a Mr. Roth in Las Vegas," and he read her the number off the card.

"He's very busy, Mr. Roth is, you don't have to call him."

"Oh, but I want to," Arnold Wylie said.

Escalante shifted in his chair, pulled at his collar again, stared out the window. The weather was clearing, spots of blue visible now; spots of grey, really, but they would have been blue if not for the smog. In a moment, Miss Rucker's little-girl voice said, "I have Samuel Roth on the line," and Wylie pushed a button, activating his speaker phone, sat back and said, "This is Arnold Wylie in Los Angeles."

"Yes?"

"Do you employ a Franklin Gambino?"

Now a pause. "You mean Franky? I do, why, is there a problem?"

Another pause, this time Wylie's. "No."

"Then why are you calling me, Mr. Wylie?"

"Just double-checking some things, Mr. Roth."

A sigh. "You're not the first one that's done this, Mr. Wylie, and I don't blame you a bit. Part of it has to do with Franky's Italianate name and part of it is that terrible slurred speech. I personally sometimes find it hard to believe he graduated third in his class at the University of Chicago Business School."

Escalante listened to Pinky's voice on the speaker phone, wondering why Pinky didn't let him be valedictorian.

"It's really quite a brilliant mind—I wish it came with a somewhat more refined exterior. But then, we can't have everything. Lee Iacocca was in here yesterday and there are still a lot of rough edges on Lee, but look at the job he's done."

"Yes," Wylie said. "You couldn't be more right."

"Is there anything else I can do for you, Mr. Wylie?"

"Not just now, and I'm sorry if I bothered you."

"No bother. Good-bye, Mr. Wylie." Pinky hung up.

"He never says nice things like that when I'm around, I'm going to hit him for a raise first thing," Escalante said.

"I'm sorry I didn't trust you totally, but you've got to understand, your appearance here was a bit unusual."

"Well, sometimes that's the price of being aggressive. Just go in and boom, get the customer's interest."

"You have my interest, Mr. Gambino."

"Okay—this is just a 'sploratory trip, you understand, so I haven't got an official proposal laid out, you know, all the dots and crosses, 'cause if you didn't want to go in with us, what would be the point?"

"How much money are your clients interested in investing?"

"Ballpark figure? For openers? Seven figures easy, and if it works, if you pick some companies that take off, we could go very heavy. You said you been to Vegas a lot. I guess you gamble. Our clients are willing to gamble with you."

The intercom sounded and then Miss Rucker's voice: "You told me to remind you of your next appointment."

Wylie blinked, thanked her. "Let me see the proposal as soon as it's ready," he told Escalante. He looked at his watch. "I'm late, I have to dash."

"Can I give you a lift?"

Wylie escorted him to the door. "I'm capable of driving myself. Good-bye, Mr. Gambino."

"You'll have the proposal before you can say Jackie Robinson, Mr. Wylie."

Wylie nodded.

Escalante took his shot then. "You say you come a lot to Vegas on business—you come on pleasure, too, I guess. Which was it yesterday?"

"I didn't say I was there yesterday."

"I know but I thought I saw you in one of the hotels. 'Course, I didn't know it was you then."

Wylie looked at him a moment before nodding. "It so happens I *was* there yesterday. My reasons will have to stay my own."

Escalante left him then, walked past Miss Rucker's desk, hoped she didn't catch his excitement when he said goodbye. And he was excited: The first decent thing that had happened to him in Los Angeles had just happened to him—because whoever sent the second kidnap note, the one with the finger in cellophane, had sent it yesterday. To Paxton. From Vegas.

At 3:10, Escalante sat in his rented car, waiting for Arnold Wylie. He had positioned himself so that he had a clear look at both the front door of Wylie's building and its garage. There was no overpoweringly logical reason to follow the man except that of the people he had met in L.A., only Wylie might have sent the notes. Which was why he had taken the shot about Wylie's visiting Vegas. There was no one else.

Whoever sent them had to be three things: broke, crazed and desperate. Miranda had a daughter but she was far too rich and much too strung out to concentrate on anything for long. And her husband knew nothing of Paxton or her pregnancy, was too busy dancing on his Hawaiian sands. Rainbeaux had a daughter, too, but she also had an I.Q. that barely reached two figures, and then only if the moon was right, so she hardly qualified as a menace to anyone. And her record-producer lover was dead.

Leaving Wylie.

Dislikable, sadistic, arrogant, probably, in the dusk of whatever soul he had left, desperate. But he didn't seem broke—he had just flushed Escalante from his office when the subject was millions of dollars. And crazy?

Unlikely.

Except his next appointment that he "had to dash" to sounded important, more than just having your poodle trimmed.

3:15.

Bright and sunny now in L.A. Escalante shifted his view

from the garage to the front of the building, eyes flicking continually.

At 3:20 he began to wonder if Wylie had gotten past him somehow. At 3:25 he decided that Wylie *must* have gotten past him somehow.

At 3:30 he decided to find out. He parked, got out of his car, used the nearest pay phone to dial Wylie's office, got not Miss Rucker but an answering machine.

Escalante put the phone back into its cradle, wondering why he had chosen now to start suddenly to perspire. He went to the office building elevators, pushed Wylie's floor and when he got there, moved silently to the office that said simply "A. Wylie" on the outside.

Escalante took off his watch, held the leather strap in one hand. He folded the buckle back, took hold of the tongue, the piece of metal that goes through the strap holes. He had filed his so that it was particularly thin, particularly sharp. He raked the tongue against the door lock two times, turned the handle, moved inside, past Miss Rucker's empty desk.

Wylie's office door was open; beyond came a slapping sound. Then Miss Rucker's baby voice: "You bastard."

Again, the slapping sound.

"Gutless bastard."

Now Wylie, voice hoarse, throat dry, the tone not the one he had used in the meeting: "Ugly freak."

Another slap.

Escalante stood frozen, and he had known men before who got off by beating up women, and he knew Wylie had that in him, Rainbeaux had said he'd beaten her up some when he was convinced Paxton had fathered their child, and part of him wanted to burst in and help the oversized Miss Rucker and another part told him to get out, now, before events got really bad, but if Wylie was crazy he had to find out and there was something crazy going on beyond the door and some things you can see every day for a lifetime and they never really register, while others you can catch for half a blink and you know, no matter how you try, the sight will be always with you, tattooed behind your eyeballs, and what he glimpsed next as he moved into position for a flick of the interior of the room was going to be the latter, because Wylie wore his tie and his vest and his jacket, but what had shifted was his trousers and his underwear, they were down around his ankles as he sat at his desk chair while the giant Miss Rucker, naked from the waist up, stood directly over him, whipping her breasts across his face, slapping back and forth.

Escalante moved out of the way, riveted as the unnatural game went dangerously on—"You love it that I'm ugly—" "Hate it—hate you"—slap—"You love it and you love me—" "Love Rainbeaux, she's beautiful—"—slap—slap—"*I'm* beautiful—say it—" "—no—" "*—SAY IT—*" "—never—" "—then I'm going, right now, I'm getting out and you better believe it—" slap—slap—"don't—" "—don't what? *—don't what?—*" "—leave me—" "—why not?—" "—because—" "*—because why?—*" slap*—slap—slap!—* "—because I love you—" "why do you love me?—" "because—because you're beautiful—so beautiful—and I love you—" "—and you hate her—" "—yes—hate her*—yes—*"

Escalante headed fast for the door as the voices got rhythmically louder along with the slapping, and before his hand was on the knob he knew that as well as "desperate," Wylie easily qualified for "crazy," "broke" he'd have to find out about, and the last thing he heard as he left them behind was Wylie, bursting into tears, crying and coming, coming and crying, both at the very same time. . . .

The phone was picked up on the first ring. "Cyrus Kinnick here."

"It's me, I'm in L.A., can you do me something?"

"Anything. Anything."

Escalante sat in his room at the Wilshire, stared out the window. It was 4:00, and the rain had reappeared. "I'm not sure if you can, but it's worth the try: You said to me you started a company yourself and sold out a few years later, computer stuff."

"Absolutely."

"Okay, here's the question: That start-up money, was it yours, or did you get it from your folks, or—"

"—my folks?—are you serious?—I told you what they were, the scum they were—shit, if they'd had it they'd have thrown it away before they gave a cent of it to me—I got it the same way everybody does in computers."

"Let me guess—you went to a venture capitalist."

"Right. Massachusetts is the second biggest state in computer companies, right after California. I got my loan, got rich, but not as rich as the guy who gave me the loan."

"You're still friendly with the guy."

"Sure."

"Okay—I'm going to guess these guys, if they don't know each other, at least they've heard about their competitors."

"I can't say, Mr. Escalante."

"All right, here's the favor: Can you contact your man and find out about a Californian named Arnold Wylie? Offices in Century City."

"Find out what?"

"I'll take what I can, but ideally? How is he doing? Is he overextended? Or in debt? And by how much? A million and a half wouldn't upset me. Do you think your man could know that?"

"It's a long shot. I'll try him. If he knows, I'm sure he'll tell me. Want me to call you in Los Angeles?"

"There's a six-thirty back to Vegas—I'll be on it—let me call you—"

"Mr. Escalante?"

"What?"

"Is this an adventure or something you're on? I mean, we're on."

"Would that make you happy?"

"Oh, yes."

"Then, that's what it is, Duke; then, that's what it is." He hung up, almost smiled as he listened to the rain. He started packing then, got halfway finished, went back to the phone, called Paxton. "Is Ashley in the room or can you talk?" he said when Paxton answered.

"Ashley's upstairs. She's angry at me about my secrets."

"Well, maybe it'll all be over soon. I think I've got the guy, I'll be back in town in a couple of hours, I'll know for sure then. Maybe."

"Let's hope so—why the 'maybe,' Nicholas?"

"I'm having a quick financial check done on the guy. An associate of mine is into it now."

"Who? I don't want the world knowing my affairs."

"His name's Cyrus Kinnick and he might be able to get some quick answers—and he doesn't *know* anything about why he's doing what I've asked him to do."

And then Paxton exploded— "I only came to you because you could be trusted—and now you betray me with . . . with this *Kinnick* person—I'm very put out with you, Nicholas—you should have inquired of me before you brought in anybody else—in this world, it's impossible to know who is trustworthy or not—"

"—go easy," Escalante interrupted. "How the hell do I know if *you*'re trustworthy or not?"

Paxton took a pause and when he spoke again, his voice was almost under control. "I'm sorry, it's been a bad time, Ashley causes such concern, I should be grateful to you that my troubles are almost over. And I am." He took a deep breath. "This person you suspect, Nicholas—why is he doing it?"

"I'm not positive yet that he is. If I'm right, I'll drive over later and explain it all to you."

"But why do you think?"

"Money and true love—and believe me, I'm shuddering as I say that, good-bye, Darryl." He hung up, finished packing, lay down on the bed.

4:15.

He closed his eyes, saw Miranda, this morning's Miranda, naked and emaciated, lying alongside him. He opened his eyes, concentrated, banished her. He closed his eyes again. Now Wylie was sitting, half naked, being beaten, in his office chair. Escalante got out of bed, began to pace. The rain had turned torrential. Fucking town. He was actually anxious to get back to Vegas.

Of course The Glider would be there, waiting. Probably these were his last hours, last six, eight, whatever. He shrugged. At least he'd be the hell out of L.A. He cocked his head, asked himself something: Was death actually preferable to Los Angeles?

Good question. . . .

# CHAPTER 3

# The Glider Sends a Message

Kinnick was waiting for him as he got off the plane, dressed in his usual Ivy costume, blazer, striped tie, and looked, if anything, more storklike than usual. He also kept shifting his weight from one foot to the other, all the while scratching his Arafat beard. Probably, Escalante decided, Kinnick's way of trying not to show excitement. "You said you'd try and catch this plane."

"So I did."

"Well, I figured, what the hell, I might as well meet you."

"Then I take it you have news."

Kinnick was almost hopping now. "I might," he managed with an attempt at what might have been casualness. "And then again, I might not."

They started through the Vegas airport on the moving sidewalk. As they went along the recorded voice of Don Rickles made a bad joke and told them to keep to the right, then the voice of Shecky Greene gave the same advice, preceded by a different joke, different but equally bad. The Joan Rivers recording was stuck; she just kept saying, "This is Joan Rivv—this is Joan Rivv—this is Joan Rivv—" and Escalante was reminded of a Billy Wilder picture where the commies tortured the young hero by playing "Eeentsee weentsee teenie weenie yellow polka dot bikini" over and over until the hero cracked.

"Aren't you even interested?" Kinnick said. "Aren't you going to tell me to go on?"

Escalante was about to tell him, but as Joan Rivers's voice grew softer behind them, he saw up ahead, standing by the moving sidewalk, an elegant man half turned away and it had to be The Glider, and as Escalante froze, the man turned, pistol in hand, except by the time the turn was finished it was no pistol, just a pipe, and the man didn't have even a second-cousin's resemblance to The Glider.

Silently, Escalante cursed his growing imagination.

"Well?" from Kinnick.

"I'm sorry. Really. Go on."

"Well, I called Max Felix in Boston. He's a little Buddha of a guy, he even blinks in slow motion. He's the guy lent me the money."

"What did he tell you?"

"I never said I got through to him. Maybe I did, and maybe I didn't."

"Oh, Jesus, Ace, cut the games."

"Well, goddammit, show a little interest, this is all new to me."

"I'm interested, believe that." It was true. The right answer from Kinnick, he could see Paxton, close things out nice and clean, no loose ends to worry over when The Glider really came.

"Okay. I got Max—"

"—and you asked him about Wylie—"

"—that's not how things go with Max—he likes to circle—you schmooze—how are things? why haven't you called me more often? why don't we go into business together again? don't you trust me? weren't we good for each other? It takes a while. Sometimes he gets so wound up he thinks *he* called *you*. I hung tough and then I hit him with the name you gave, Arnold Wylie."

They were at the airport doors now. Escalante had traveled under the seat and he hesitated a moment before going out into the night, hailing a cab. The weather had changed—it was coming up Christmas fast now but the night air was remarkably warm. They waited, a dozen people ahead of them in the rush for taxis.

"What did he say?"

"Two words: 'That prick.'"

Escalante could feel himself breathing more easily. "Go on."

"You don't want to hear it all, but just to bottom-line it, Wylie was crooked in a deal with Max—at least Max thinks he was—I'm talking twenty years ago but Max remembers double-crosses, things like that—and he's kept close tabs on Wylie—"

"And—Jesus, Kinnick, come on!"

Kinnick smiled. "Wylie got caught a couple years ago investing in starting up some video game companies. He was in pretty heavy—this was just before the Atari disaster, and all that."

Escalante grabbed Kinnick by the blazer: "So he's in deep, right?"

Kinnick kind of smiled, then nodded. "This is none of it exact—but Max says at least a million. The quote is 'More than one but maybe less than two, goddammit.' Max wouldn't mind a lot if Wylie went under."

Escalante said nothing. He let Kinnick go, took a breath. It was, as much as it would ever be, over. A kidnap note asks for one and a half million dollars. A strange amount—you demand one million, you demand five, no one demanded one and a half.

Unless he was in debt that much.

What he had to do now was tell Paxton. And Paxton would have to decide what moves to make next. A cab stopped. They got in. "Did I do good?" Kinnick asked.

"You were flawless. Where can I drop you?"

"Where you going?"

"My place, to get out of these clothes, then I have a visit to make."

Kinnick practically began bouncing up and down on the seat. "You're going to your *home* and you want to get rid of me? I do fucking perfect for you and I never even ask why I'm doing it and you deprive me of a chance to see your home? Do you know how I've thought about it—when I checked on you I kept coming up zip on your home, but, Jesus, how can you not let me see your gym—I figure you must have a fabulous gym, you know, for working out, practicing new ways to get even stronger, and a kind of gourmet kitchen, not big necessarily, but a couple of blenders for your health food, everybody tough is into vitamins and fruit milk shakes with eggs and all kinds of shit—it wouldn't be human for you to drop me off at the Grand, not now."

"The maid hasn't been in, but what the hell," Escalante said, and he gave the address on Bonanza, in the heart of Naked City.

The thing was, Kinnick loved the place. Escalante stood in the doorway, watching as Kinnick, hands clasped together in what might have been supplication, said, "Omigod, the maps, I didn't know you knew about maps, I love maps, when I was a kid I had maps all over my room, oh, Christ, look at this, the Congo—you've got the Congo on your ceiling, Jesus—" He stared up, mouth open.

Escalante quickly changed, out of the suit and tie, into his khakis and tennis shoes and blue shirt. He went to the refrigerator, poured two Finlandias, rocks, gave one to Kinnick, who was studying the Spanish Riviera now. Together they went out onto the terrace facing Bonanza. It was getting strangely warmer now, and the street was unusually quiet, just one drunken singer had the area pretty much to himself. He was full of spirits and the spirit of the season as he sang, slowly, but with a firm bass voice, "O Holy Night," he began, "the stars are brightly something . . ."

"'Shining,' you asshole," another male voice corrected from out there in the darkness. "'The stars are brightly *shining*.'"

"Thank you ever so, dear heart," the singer replied, his sincerity clear. Then he was back to his music: "'O Holy

Night, the stars are brightly shining, it is the night of our dear Savior's girth.'"

"Not *'girth'*—" the corrector screamed. "That makes no fucking sense, man. What the fuck's our Savior's 'girth' got to do with anything? *Birth,* you asshole. *Buh. Buh.*"

Escalante smiled, was about to speak when The Glider did strike, the single shot ringing in the darkness, and Escalante made it to the floor of the terrace fast, stared as Kinnick screamed, turned, and as the blood suddenly soaked his blazer in the area above his heart, he toppled, and Escalante grabbed him as the roar of a car took The Glider away and then they were back inside the room and Escalante ripped the tie from Kinnick's throat, removed the blazer with the shoulder holster and the gun nestled inside and there was little resistance or movement from Kinnick as Escalante at last tore away the shirt, stared at the emaciated hairless body with the blood pouring free. Even before he'd removed the shirt, Escalante was already stunned, but nothing he had ever known prepared him for what he realized next—there were terrible scars surrounding Kinnick's breasts. Christ alone knew how many stitches. And the flesh was still, as it always would be, a deep and horrid red. Mastectomies were not without their stigmata.

And Cyrus Kinnick had once been a girl.

It was after ten when the two cars arrived at the Paxton house. Escalante, in the lead car, pulled into the driveway while the Frog Prince and the two other men stayed out on the street. "I don't think I'll keep you waiting long," Escalante said, and he walked to the front door, knocked.

Paxton answered almost immediately. "You don't look well, Nicholas," he said. "Is something the matter?"

"Yes."

"Good heavens, we must talk about it, then," and they went inside, to the living room. Escalante had been there before, but never late like this, and the religious paintings stood out beautifully, the lights accenting the eyes of the Madonnas, the Christs, the many children. They sat in chairs, facing each other.

"Where's Ashley?"

Paxton smiled. "I know you have a weak stomach for this kind of thing, Nicholas, but Ashley's upstairs as we speak, praying for me. You see, earlier this evening, when she was in such anguish about what she felt were the secrets destroying us, I reached a decision I know now I should have come to long ago. You said it yourself, Nicholas: You cannot shield another human, no one can be totally protected. So I told her of my indiscretions in Los Angeles. And, thank the Lord, she forgave me. She's praying for my sins, Nicholas. And for the first time in such a long time, she's totally at peace. As am I. As am I."

Escalante said nothing, just studied the other man.

Paxton leaned forward then. "Whatever is the matter with me?—here you tell me you're not well and instead of asking you about it, I go prattling on about my own happiness. Forgive me. Your turn. What's wrong, Nicholas?"

"Someone tried to shoot me earlier tonight, Darryl."

"Dear God—"

"—at least I thought someone did."

Paxton looked confused. "You 'thought'? I'm not sure I quite understand you."

Ashley's voice came then from the stairwell: "Darryl?"

Paxton stood. "We're in here, darling. Nicholas has come to call."

A moment later Ashley moved into the room, went to Paxton, stood close. "Good evening, Nicholas."

Escalante nodded.

Ashley looked at him. "You didn't say 'madam.' You always say 'madam' when you see me."

"He's not himself."

"I forgive you, Nicholas. I've not been myself these last days." She smiled. "You know I know?"

Escalante nodded again.

"What *is* the matter with him?" Ashley said then. "I don't think I like his behavior."

Escalante said, "I don't like it either, Ashley—this hasn't been one of the better days."

"Earlier, someone tried to shoot him," Paxton said.

Ashley shook her head in disbelief.

"I said I thought someone did. For a while. I knew it was possible. But then just after the shooting I got to thinking—the man who was after me is a great gunman—now I know night fire is never easy. So it's possible he would have missed me. But I also knew he never would have missed me by as much as he did. That is, *if* he was aiming for me. And right now, I don't think he was. As a matter of fact, I don't think he even did the shooting." Escalante rubbed his eyes. "What do you think, Darryl?"

"What do *I* think? Obviously, that you've had a terrible experience."

"And that's all? I think there's something else, Darryl—and I wish you'd talk about it now."

"What else could there conceivably be? I don't know about the other parts of your life. Why anyone would want to shoot you or not. I just know that Ashley and I have spent all evening together, here, finding each other again."

Escalante sighed. "Have it your way," he said as he stood, started for the living-room entrance.

"You're leaving?"

"No. I'll be back," and he went outside then, hurried down to the second car, where Pinky and the Frog Prince waited in the front seat, Kinnick stretched out, breathing softly, in the back. "I'll take him now," Escalante said as he opened the rear door.

The Frog Prince got out to help. "Just remember to go very easy with him. The wound's not going to reopen, I've handled gunshots before. But he's lost a lot of blood. And he's goddam lucky no bones were hit. He needs to rest, Mex."

"He needs this more. And I'll lie him down inside." He

reached out, spoke softly. "Come on, Ace, we've got some people to see."

Kinnick blinked. Whatever pills the Frog Prince had given him were working on the pain. Pinky opened the other rear door. It took the three of them to maneuver Kinnick out of the car without undue hurt. Once he was out, Escalante took him.

"Want us to wait?"

"No need."

"We'll head on home, then," Pinky said. "We had a real breakthrough earlier today."

"That's right," the Frog Prince said. "Pinky found the last flaw in our roulette system, we've been making a mistake with the double zero but we've just about got it solved now. We'll be Concordeing out of here before you know it."

Escalante looked at the two of them. "I wish you such joy," he said, and then he carefully guided Kinnick along the walk toward the Paxton house.

". . . cold . . ." Kinnick said. He was dressed as before, same slacks, same blazer with the gun and holster inside, but he was wearing a different shirt, one of Froggie's.

"Want me to carry you?"

Nod.

Escalante lifted him gently, moved inside, closed the front door, stood in the entrance to the living room. "Forgive me for this," he said, "I hate surprises and I'm sure you do, too, but this is the young man I told you about on the phone, Darryl, Cyrus Kinnick, he's into adventure and he's had a rough day, I thought we might cheer him. Cyrus, this is the Reverend Darryl Paxton and Ashley, his wife." He was at the sofa by this time and he knelt, carefully stretched Kinnick along the cushions, got him as comfortable as he could.

In the room: dead silence.

Escalante sat, wondered if the human ear could monitor emotions, how loud would be the cries of shock, remorse and pain. He looked at the three of them. He hadn't wanted to force the confrontation but Darryl wouldn't talk when he'd come in alone. Escalante looked at Darryl now. He did not appear to give the impression of breathing. Escalante studied Ashley next, watched her as her face came apart and for a moment he thought she was having a spasm but it wasn't that; she was just attacking her blue eyes with her fingers, would have really dug in except that Darryl got to her, forced her fists down to her sides, held her that way until he thought it was safe.

When he finally let her go, there was the silence again, until Ashley began to sob. Her hands still down, she shook her head as the tears poured. "...you said we were free of him...you promised..."

From Paxton: "...I thought we were...I thought we were..."

Kinnick spoke at last. "...never..."

Ashley's sobbing became more intense.

Darryl tried to "there-there" her, promised her everything would be wonderful, pleaded with her to stop.

"I don't believe your promises, not anymore; there'll be no 'wonderfuls' for us, Darryl."

"There, there, love; there, there."

"Thirty years ago you called me 'love' and pleaded with me to open my legs. And I loved you back, so I did." She turned to Kinnick now. "And twenty-nine years ago you were born." The tears had her again. "And how glorious our lives have been."

"Ah, beloved," Darryl said. "There, there."

Kinnick looked at Escalante then. "Isn't it wonderful, watching them suffer...?"

"No."

"...I've dreamt of it...for six years...when I saw them on the Donahue show...he was doing the talking but the cameras showed her face...and as soon as I saw I knew...we looked so alike we could have been sisters...I didn't look like this then...I hadn't begun the change...and I called the show...I got through...I told people I was family, that wasn't a lie...when she came on I said who I was and that I loved her...but she got hysterical and hung up...I couldn't believe it...all my life I'd been the best girl, a perfect girl, because I knew...someday I'd find my real parents and when I did, I wanted for them to be so proud of me...and after she hung up, I flew here...I got in to see them...I said 'Here I am, it's really me'...and they threw me out, they said they had no children...I begged them...I'd been searching for them, some part of me had, all my life...and when I finally found them...they scorned me...twice they scorned me...first when they gave me away and then when I found them...I told them someday I'd come back to punish them...I had to punish them...just like they'd punished me..."

"Would you ever have left us alone?" Paxton said.

"...oh, God, never...I would have kept writing notes and kept writing notes...and then someday, when you were crazy with fear, I was going to do what you feared most...tell the world...I wanted the world to know what sinners you were...how you claimed to love children but hated your own...public humiliation...that was my gift for you...."

"I knew you'd never stop," Paxton said. "I knew that someone had to try and stop you."

Escalante looked at the three Paxtons and there was such suffering in the room. Thirty years ago a cock had spurted sperm and Darryl and Ashley, so overconfident of their own Goodness, could never forgive their own normal desires, could never forget the ensuing shame.

The fighting Paxtons, he thought, reminding himself that fighting was, for some, a form of intimacy, and he wondered what kind of animals they would become when they were left alone to deal with each other. Because some animals, like wolves, those equipped with the ability to kill their food, have a built-in reluctance to use their killing power on each other. While animals who are equipped to flee, like turtledoves, have no such inhibitions. And the Paxton men had weapons.

Wolves or turtledoves?

Escalante looked at Darryl, whose deepest "sin" until tonight had been a desire to be inside the woman he loved. He looked at Kinnick, stretched out, staring at them, his eyes wide and bright, the eyes close in color to Ashley's. And Ashley herself, the tears drying now, whose parents had wanted a son and now had a son of her own in the room with her.

Turtledoves or wolves?

However they decided, the decision could only be theirs—he had been too much with them, knew secrets no outsider should ever know. Christ, the way the world had toppled in the last few hours. Way back then, his mind was on a man named Arnold Wylie who he thought might be the madman, but once the shot was fired, once he realized that Kinnick might be someone's dumpling of a daughter and that The Glider would never have missed, everything was scratched clean. Something had happened to the Paxtons thirty years ago, and Kinnick was the right age to have been that something. And Kinnick had an almost uncontrollable anger toward his parents. And Paxton had exploded on the telephone when Escalante mentioned Kinnick's name.

He hoped that Kinnick's anger would dissolve and disappear. Along with Ashley's fears and Darryl's guilts. But that was beyond his power to control. He stood quietly, started out of the room.

"Where are you going?" Paxton said suddenly. "Are you going to the police?"

"Why would I do that, Darryl? I don't have any real proof. And it's not any of my business. My business was to find out who sent the notes and that we've done. I don't like the police a whole lot. And I do like the three of you.

You're all really very nice people. You just have a problem getting along with each other. But that's your problem; believe it or not, I have several of my own."

And then he left them and was gone, from the room, the house, their lives. He got quickly into his car, backed down the driveway, shifted out of reverse, drove away, and as he did he heard, or thought he heard, from somewhere behind him in the night, an explosive sound. Backfire? Gunshot? He couldn't be sure, but whatever it was, it was history.

Nothing so unusual about that, he was going to be history, too, probably soon, and when he got to the coffee shop of the Silver Spoon, Roxy was on, working a double shift, looking punchy, and he headed toward table seventy-five, was barely seated when she signaled for him, holding the receiver in one hand, and when he went to her she said, "You've been getting called every few minutes," and he only wondered what it was for a moment until he heard The Glider's voice going, "It's me, darlin'. Actor story. Young friend of mine here in Tahoe, longed to be a great Shakespearean, and, I don't have to tell you, the opportunities in Nevada for that kind of employment are a bit on the limited side but then he got a last-minute call—a play was being done starting in less than an hour, and would he play a part, they asked, and he said 'I can't learn a part in an hour' and they said 'It's only one line: *Hark, is that a cannon I hear?*' and my young friend, thrilled at the opportunity so suddenly thrust at him, said he would love to play the part and he raced to the theater, thinking in his mind of his one line: *Hark, is that a cannon I hear?* and when he got backstage it was near to curtain time and they quick fitted him for a costume and slapped some makeup on his face and all he was thinking while this was going on was his one line, *Hark, is that a cannon I hear?* and then they were leading him toward the wings and the curtain was up, the play had started, actors rushing to and fro, and then at the proper moment for his entrance they pushed him on stage and the instant he got there, there was a huge explosion and he turned and shouted *'What the fuck was that?'* "

Escalante listened to The Glider's laugh. It was filled with effort.

"Don't tell me you've heard it, I know you've heard it, I've told you myself a dozen times alone. But there's a point to it tonight. And it's this: You won't be hearing *my* cannon, Nikki, we shall not be meeting at Samarra, the wife did what women are best at, and you know what that is."

"Bet you'll tell me."

"She doesn't want to go to Mexico; she changed her mind. I pleaded but no point. She wants to die in her own bed. Have you ever heard such a clichéd thing?"

"I'd settle."

*"You mustn't."*

The upset was clear in the older man's voice now and Escalante waited. The Glider always began with a story; his intention would be coming next.

"I called DeMarco—I explained I would not be needing the seventy-five—he said it didn't matter, that he thought all the time I'd turn coward, that you'd be dead by morning anyway, so I've been calling you and calling you—to warn you—Nikki, Nikki, Nikki, you were in bad shape when we had coffee but you must get a grip—*DeMarco must not take you.* You must go someplace. You must hide until you're yourself again."

"I'm not up to running, I don't want to hide."

"You have to."

"Oh? Where is that written?" Escalante said good-bye then, hung up, walked to table seventy-five, grunted thanks when Roxy brought him his coffee, a roll and butter, left him in peace, and he sat still for a while, wondering when DeMarco and his men would come for him—

—and it was then, precisely then, at 11:21 P.M. that he realized they weren't going to come for him. They were already there. For at that moment DeMarco himself moved into the coffee-shop doorway with a smile plastered on his Stallone face, and as Escalante watched he realized that the two large men seated several tables to his left were watching DeMarco, too, as were the two men seated several tables to his right.

Jesus, five of them, and he was dead in the middle, and would they shoot him here?—in a coffee shop on the Strip of one of the best hotels in town?—

—interesting questions, yes, and the answers certainly had more than a little meaning to him, but there was no law that said he had to wait to find out, so he leaned back in his chair, hesitated, then intentionally let the balance go and as the chair crashed he rolled out of it and behind table seventy-five was the kitchen area and he raced there now, conscious of the cries behind him and soon there were shouts all around him as the kitchen help let themselves be heard from—

—Escalante ran—he didn't go all out because he'd never been in the kitchen before and sure, they'd blast him here but only if they caught him and what he needed more than full speed was the knowledge of where the exit was and when he at last saw it he increased his pace, blasted out of the door into the night, looked left, right, left again, because he was on the side of the building now, not far from where he'd had a talk just the afternoon before with the Frog Prince and now Escalante let it all out, everything he had, running toward the unused entrance on the side of the Silver Spoon and more than the entrance, toward the cement overhang that he and Froggie had talked beneath, and it was ten feet up but he could reach it, if he timed it right, and there was going to be no second shot and it was dark but there it was, the overhang, and he leaped for it, grabbed it, swung his body up and over, then lay flat on top, hidden in the darkness, safe.

Safe?

He heard them. Their voices. DeMarco's the loudest.

Coming in his direction. He tried to press his body almost into the cement. He lay flat and still, hoping they would not hear him breathe.

Had they seen him?

Doubtful. Their voices as they came on and on were too full of questions. He could not make out the exact words yet, but their sentences had rising inflections at the ends.

They came closer, moving always steadily toward beneath where he lay hidden. He held his breath. If he made no sound he'd be all right.

"All right" might be overstating it a bit. Five men were out to kill him. And he was hiding in the darkness, praying to be able to control his own breathing.

What was it he'd just said to The Glider? That he wouldn't run and that he wouldn't hide? Whatever it was he was doing was a pretty good imitation.

Now they were directly beneath him, standing where he and Froggie had stood. DeMarco was cursing them. For letting the spick get away. Escalante listened as, a few feet below, DeMarco went on with his harangue, saying few good things about him.

I don't want to hear this, Escalante thought, so he closed his eyes and DeMarco's anger was hard not to listen to, so he decided to travel somewhere, go someplace he loved, and the Annapurna gorge seemed a likely spot, he'd been there recently but the yellow of the sunset was always worth another try, so Escalante went there—

—only the mountain wasn't yellow this time. It was red. The mountain was blood. Escalante opened his eyes and felt it begin to happen, felt the heat start in his groin as his reptile brain decided to assert itself.

The five men were moving now, out from beneath the overhang, and he could see their guns, Magnums and Berettas, some with silencers, some not, all five heavily armed—

—with bubble-gum weapons!

*He* was the one with true power . . . he held his coffee spoon in one hand, a butter knife in the other. Enough to bring a battalion down. He closed his eyes again, saw the same red, but deeper now, and the heat was increasing as he carefully moved into a kneeling position, looked at the five men.

What was it Holly had asked him as they said good-bye? Something like "You could take five, couldn't you, Mex?"

And he said what? "Not happily."

How could he have been so wrong? The growing heat inside him, that brought joy along with it. Now he began, silently, to stand. It should all be over fast. If he was still the most lethal man alive. Was he? Time to find out. The next minute would tell. Once it would have lasted, at the most, sixty seconds. (This time it took forty-two.) With DeMarco saved for last. (DeMarco went last.) He dropped on them then like a curse from heaven.

His nuts felt on fire. . . .